S0-AJL-508

G2234 ri
3 0250 00450 1990

Also by Doris Gates

LITTLE VIC

MY BROTHER MIKE

NORTH FORK

TROUBLE FOR JERRY

SENSIBLE KATE

BLUE WILLOW

SARAH'S IDEA

River Ranch

by Doris Gates

Illustrated by Jacob Landau

New York THE VIKING PRESS 1951

FIRST PUBLISHED BY THE VIKING PRESS IN OCTOBER 1949

PUBLISHED ON THE SAME DAY IN THE DOMINION OF CANADA

BY THE MACMILLAN COMPANY OF CANADA LIMITED

SECOND PRINTING SEPTEMBER 1951

PRINTED IN THE UNITED STATES OF AMERICA

BY THE VAIL-BALLOU PRESS, INC., BINGHAMTON, N. Y.

Contents

River Ranch

CHAPTER ONE

Ben's Night Ride

IT WAS very dark and still. Ben rode slowly across the corral to the barn. The only sound was the jingle of the bit chains on his pony's head. The horse was glad to be home again. He walked faster and nodded his head up and down.

Ben pulled up and stopped the pony at the open barn door. He swung out of the saddle. The pony started to walk into the barn.

"Take it easy," said Ben. "Your hay is there waiting for you. It won't run away."

The pony bumped his head against Ben's back. He liked Ben, and he could almost understand what he said. He and Ben had been friends for many years. Ben had taught him all that a good cow pony should know. He had been a wild horse when Ben had roped him and broken him to the saddle. Ben had named him "Pilot" because he had been a leader of the wild horse herd. But most of the time Ben called him "Pie" for short.

Ben led Pie into the barn. Several horses stirred in their stalls. In the dark, they were trying to see who was coming in. They seemed to know it was Ben and Pie. They became quiet again while Ben put Pie into his own stall and took off the pony's saddle.

Pie at once began to eat the good hay which he had not had time to finish when Ben had come for him. Ben gave him a pat on his smooth black neck.

"Good boy, Pilot," Ben said. "I'll be seeing you."

Then Ben went out of the barn. He did not shut

the door because the night was very warm. Over his head the stars were big and bright in the dark sky. In front of him was the ranch house. He saw a light in the kitchen window.

"Good," he said to himself. "Ann is up. Perhaps she has fixed a sandwich for me."

Ben and Pilot had traveled many miles this night. Like Pilot, Ben was hungry. He was also very tired.

Ann was busy at the stove when Ben came into the kitchen.

"Hello," she said, turning toward him with a smile. "Take off your shooting iron and sit down. I thought you could maybe do with a bite to eat."

"I sure could," said Ben. He took off the belt that held his gun, and laid it on the table.

"How did you know when I'd be home?" he asked.

Ann laughed. "I didn't really. I woke up all of a sudden. Something told me you were gone. When I went into your room to see, sure enough, you were. Your sheets were cold, so I knew you had been gone for quite a while. I couldn't go back to sleep again, so I came down here to wait for you. I just guessed about when I should start getting your supper ready."

"You mean breakfast," Ben said. "It is three o'clock in the morning."

While they were talking, Ann moved back and forth across the big ranch kitchen. She put Ben's food on the table. There was a pile of sandwiches, as well as something hot to drink. Ben took a big bite of sandwich while Ann sat across the table watching him. She was wishing he would talk about his night ride. But Ben was too hungry to talk just yet. For several minutes Ann did not say a word. She let him finish one whole sandwich. When he reached out for the second one, she could wait no longer.

"Did you see them?" she asked.

Ben shook his head. His mouth was too full for talking. Ann's dark eyes searched his face while she wondered how he could want to eat with so much going on. Boys were funny animals, she thought, even when they were your own brothers.

Ben took another big bite and looked at Ann. His eyes were full of fun. He knew how his sister felt. Ben and Ann were very good friends. He thought her the most wonderful sister in the world. And she thought her big brother could do no wrong. Now that she had turned fifteen, they enjoyed doing things together, though Ben, who was twenty, still thought of Ann as a child.

Just now she looked like a little girl. Her dark hair hung in two short pigtails that brushed her shoulders. She had on an old blue housecoat that was too small for her. It had been a Christmas present the year she was twelve, and now her thin arms stuck out of its sleeves, and it was much too short. Ann was growing tall, but she was still thin—"skinny" was what Ben said. But she looked fine in jeans, which she liked to wear better than dresses. They went well, too, with her turned-up nose and lively dark eyes. In short, Ann looked like the kind of girl who belongs on a cattle ranch. And that is just where she wanted to belong.

"Fred is still out looking for them," Ben said at last.

"Then you *did* see them."

"No, we didn't see them, but we saw where they had been. We found where they had killed three head of cattle and dressed the meat under the trees near the bridge. We found the hides, and there were footprints along with the tracks of the truck tires going in and out."

Ann drew in her breath and her eyes got very round. "Cattle thieves," she whispered. "Just like in the old days."

"Yes," said Ben, "only now they get around in fast trucks, and they are a lot harder to catch than in the old days."

"Of course it *would* have to happen when Dad and Mom are away," Ann said.

Ben set his mouth tight, and his eyes looked angry.

"That's just why they are working now. They have found out in some way that Dad is gone and that I am taking care of the ranch. They wouldn't dare to come fooling around here if Dad was home."

He looked so unhappy that Ann reached out and laid a hand on his arm. "You know that is not so," she said. "Dad could not do any more than you are doing."

"Well, one thing is sure," said Ben. "Fred and I alone won't be able to catch them. We need a whole bunch of riders."

"I know what," said Ann suddenly. "While you are sleeping today, I'll ride over to the Bar-B Ranch and ask them to help us."

Ben looked at her with new interest. "That's not a bad idea," he said.

They were silent for a few minutes. Then Ann said, "Do you think we should send for Dad and Mom?"

"We'll have to," Ben answered, "if this goes on much longer. But it seems too bad to call them back.

It's the first time they have had a holiday in years, and they both need it. Anyway"—here Ben rose and began to walk up and down the kitchen—"if I'm not able to run the ranch without help now, I'm never going to be able to do it. I hate to admit to Dad that I can't get along on my own. He'd certainly think he had a washout for a son if I had to go crying to him the minute he left the place."

"How many head have we lost so far?" Ann asked.

"Only seven. But we can't lose many more and come out even this year, with meat the price it is. Dad has a hard enough time without having his cattle stolen."

"You still haven't told me all that happened to-night," said Ann. "Sit down now and give. I'm just as interested in all this as you and Fred, you know. After all, I am Dad's daughter."

Ben smiled at her and went back to his chair. "All right, my child," he said, "here is what happened.

"You remember that the first night Dad and Mom were away, or anyway we thought it was that first night, the cattle thieves made their kill in the hills away from the river. I found the two hides just by chance a few days later when I happened to be riding up that way. That was the first we knew about what was going on. Then the next time they came they took two more head out of the corral in the lower pasture. Drove their truck right up to the gate and loaded it right at the spot. Well, of course Fred and I thought they would come again to one or the other of those two places. So we watched those places. I went up to the hills, and Fred hid near the corral. And what happened? The thieves did not go to either one of those places. They picked the river this time, and Fred and I had our rides for nothing."

"You had the longest ride," said Ann, as if that mattered at this time.

"That's right," said Ben. "And did I ever feel foolish."

"How did you ever find where they were tonight?"

"I had decided that they weren't going to show up

in the hills, and so I started Pie for home. As I rode down the trail, I thought I saw something flash down near the bridge. Right away I thought it might be the headlights of a truck. It wasn't far from the highway. But I was. No matter how fast I hurried Pie, I knew I never could get there soon enough to catch the thieves. And, of course, I was not even sure it was they. But I kept watching that spot and riding toward it. I kept listening for the sound of a car as I got closer. But I guess I must have spotted them the first time as they were leaving. Because I never did hear the truck. I found the tracks with my flashlight and followed them up to the place where the thieves did their killing. Then I went back and waited for Fred to ride in. When he came I told him what I had found, and we rode back together for another look around. Then I came back here, and Fred went on up along the highway to see if they had turned off anywhere. He'll be back in a little while. So now you have the story."

"I know what," said Ann soon after Ben had finished.

"What?"

"I'll go and watch one of the places next time, with you and Fred at the other two."

Ben just looked at her, and the eager light went out of Ann's eyes. "Don't be silly," said her big brother. "This is nothing for little girls to be playing around with. You just keep the house running, and we men will look after the ranch."

Ann lowered her head as if she might be hiding tears, and Ben was suddenly sorry for having spoken as he did.

"I'm sorry, Sis," he said. "I just was afraid you might get some foolish ideas into your good sound head. Don't forget it is mighty important to men to know that there will always be a good dinner ready when they get through with whatever it is they have to do. Fred and I couldn't carry on at all if you didn't keep us well fed and happy. And if anything happened to you, I would never get over it. These men carry guns, you know, just as Fred and I do."

"I know," Ann said quietly. "I'll be good, Ben. I promise."

"That's my Ann," said Ben. "Now what do you say we get some sleep before the sun gets over the hill?"

"Okay," Ann answered.

Ben put out the light, and together they left the kitchen.

CHAPTER TWO

Danger's Find

BUT BEN did not sleep all day as Ann had supposed he would after riding most of the night. He woke up with the sun streaming into his room. An angry line showed between his blue eyes when he saw how late it was.

"I was a fool not to tell Ann to call me," he said to himself as he jumped out of bed.

He dressed in a hurry and went down to the kitchen. Ann was nowhere in sight, but she had left Ben's breakfast on the back of the big kitchen stove where it could keep warm. While he was eating, Ann came in. She had been out feeding the chickens.

"Good morning, lazybones," she said. "I didn't want you to get up for hours."

"I didn't want to sleep so late," Ben answered. "Where's Fred?"

"He didn't come home last night," Ann said. "His horse is not here, so I guess he stayed all night at another ranch."

Ben pushed away his plate. "I guess so." He slid back his chair and rose. But before he left the house he belted on his big black gun.

Ann was watching him. "Where are you going, Ben?"

"I'm going to ride over to the Bar-B and ask for help. We ranchers may have to gather together in a kind of patrol before this is over."

He saw the longing in her eyes, and he shook his head. "No, you may *not* go with me. You can help a lot by just sticking close to home and sort of keeping an eye on things. No telling what these birds may do."

Ann said nothing, and Ben went outside.

He stood on the back steps for a minute and let his eyes travel slowly from east to west. His hands rested lightly on his hips. Ben was tall and his shoulders were wide. His big cowboy hat was tipped over one eye. Chaps covered his long legs. Even with all his trouble, Ben was smiling a proud smile as his eyes took in the ranch stretching out before him.

The land rose gently toward the hills which stood out against the bright morning sky. Off to the right of the ranch house and running down from the hills was a curling line of green. This was the river and the green was the trees and brush which grew along its banks. The river marked the west side of the ranch. Across it lay the land which belonged to the Bar-B outfit. Over that way, also, were the highway and the bridge. It was there, near the bridge, that the cattle thieves had made their kill last night.

As Ben's eyes reached this spot, the smile left his face and the angry line showed again between his eyes. He was mad all through as he remembered what had happened there.

Suddenly he felt a gentle rubbing against his leg and he looked down quickly. The smile was back in place at once, and Ben reached down a friendly hand.

"Hello, good-for-nothing," he said, rubbing the ears of what looked like a tame wolf. "Where were you last night when the thieves stole our cattle?"

As if to show Ben that he did not care what the man called him so long as he petted him, the great dog opened his big mouth and very gently took Ben's hand between his long white teeth.

"Would you like to trot over to the Bar-B with Pie and me, Danger? Would you?" Ben asked.

As if he could understand every word Ben was saying, Danger answered in two barks so loud that they brought Ann hurrying to the back door.

"What in the world is going on?" she asked. "I thought someone rode in."

"No," said Ben. "I just asked Danger if he would like to go over to the Bar-B with me, and he said he would."

Ann laughed. "You two!" she said. "To hear you anyone would think you could understand each other."

"We can," Ben told her. And with Danger running in wild circles around him, he started toward the horse barn.

Ann had opened the stalls when she went to feed the chickens. Now the horses were all out in the sunshine of the corral. There were four horses—Pie and three others. Fred's horse should have been there, only Fred had not come home last night.

When Pie saw Ben, he came trotting over to the corral gate. His ears were pointed toward Ben, and his big brown eyes stared hard at Ben as he came nearer.

"Come on, fellow," said Ben. "You and I are going places."

Ben opened the corral gate, and Pie followed him up to the barn door. There he waited while Ben got a brush and came back to brush Pilot's shiny black coat. Ben went carefully all over the horse. Sometimes Pie kicked and laid his ears back if Ben brushed too hard. But on the whole Pie stood the brushing very well. When Ben had looked carefully at each of Pie's feet and combed out his long wavy mane and tail, Pie threw up his head proudly and blew through his soft nose. It was as if he were trying to say, "Now I know I am the finest looking horse on the ranch." And he was!

While all this was going on, Danger sat back on his tail and watched. His red mouth was stretched wide, and all his white teeth were showing. It looked as if he were laughing at Pie. But he might have been feeling good about the coming trip with Ben. Once he gave a short bark. Ben was brushing down one of Pie's front legs and he looked over at Danger.

"What's the matter with you?" he asked the dog. "Isn't this job going fast enough to suit you?"

At this Danger closed his mouth and very slowly laid himself down in the dust of the corral with his front feet out straight before him. Then he put his nose on his paws and looked at Ben, as much as to say, "Don't be mad at me. I wouldn't hurt your feelings for the world." He looked so sad that Ben laughed, at which Danger at once sat up on his tail again and opened his mouth wide. Ben wasn't mad at him after all. It was still going to be a good day!

When Pilot was saddled and ready, Ben led him out of the corral. Danger bounced around them, barking wildly.

"Shut up," said Ben to Danger, "or I'll leave you home."

At once Danger dropped his wildly waving tail and stopped his noise. When Ben swung into the saddle and started Pie out of the ranch yard, Danger trotted quietly just behind the horse's feet. But his ears were up and his eyes were bright.

For a while Ben held Pie to a walk. Then, when he thought the horse had warmed up enough, Ben spoke to him, and Pie started off gladly in the swinging trot which cow ponies like so well. Ben knew that Pie could keep going for hours at this speed without getting too tired.

When they got to the ranch gate, Ben leaned from the saddle and opened it. They went through, and Ben edged Pilot over to it and drew it shut again. Now no loose cattle could get out on the highway. The mailbox stood on its post beside the gate. Ben stopped and looked inside. It was just about time for the mailman to come driving by. There might be a letter from Dad or Mom. But the mailbox was empty, so Ben shut it again and rode down along the side of the highway toward the bridge.

At the place where the highway ran up onto the bridge, Ben saw the tracks of an automobile or truck leading off toward the river from the highway. He turned Pie and followed where they led.

The sun was now high in the sky. But down here along the river it was cool. The music of the rushing water as it went singing over its stones was a cool sound. Grass covered the riverbank, and the bending branches of the trees brushed the stream, making shadowy places over the water. Ben knew that fish love to hide in such water, and he wished he had brought his rod along. Then he remembered. He had no time today for fishing. He must try to find out something about the cattle thieves. Overhead, in the blue sky, a big dark bird was circling. Ben thought it had come for some of the leftovers from the killing last night. Thinking of that, he hurried Pilot's speed, and they went flying over the ground. Danger came bounding alongside.

Under the trees at the water's edge Ben got off his horse and tied him loosely to a bit of brush. Danger was nosing the ground ahead of him, where a pile of something dark showed in the spots of sunlight. Slowly Ben walked over to where Danger was sniffing. At his feet was a dark and smelly heap of skins. Kicked to one side of the unpleasant heap were the heads of three shorthorn cattle. Their white faces and short dark horns stood out against the red hides beside which they were lying. Ben stooped and, while Danger watched him closely, stretched out a hide, holding it by the long red tail. Sure enough, there was the River Ranch brand—two R's placed close together. Ben said something under his breath which his mother would not have liked at all. Then he threw the hide from him. Its tail, swinging out in a crazy circle, almost struck Danger on the nose. The dog growled and backed a few steps. Danger, it seemed, didn't like the looks of things any more than Ben did.

While Ben got down on his knees to look more closely at the car tracks which were pressed into the soft earth, Danger went sniffing off on his own. The tracks were perfectly smooth. Not very safe tires for wet weather, Ben thought. Either they were very worn, or else the faces of the tires had been filled so the markings in the rubber would not give them away.

"Very clever," said Ben. "Very clever indeed!"

Ben had got to his feet again and was moving toward the spot where Pie was tied when he felt

something cold and wet hit his hand. He looked down, and there was Danger, holding something in his mouth. His tail was waving slowly and his head was held high. It was plain that Danger was very proud of himself.

Ben put out his hand. "Here, boy," he said, "give it here."

Carefully Danger laid on Ben's open hand a pipe for smoking. Its bowl was empty, but the tube the smoke came through showed that it had had much use. It was clean and looked well cared for. Plainly this pipe belonged to someone who had been here not so very long ago. Ben closed his hand over it and looked around quickly. No one was in sight. He looked again at the hides under the trees. Who had lost this pipe? Had it belonged to one of the thieves who had been here last night? Or did it belong to someone else, a fisherman perhaps, who had dropped it as he bent over to bait his hook? Ben didn't know the answer, of course. But he had a feeling deep inside him that when he knew that answer he would be on the track of the men who had killed seven head of River Ranch cattle.

"Good boy," he said to Danger as he bent over to pat his wide head. "Good boy."

Then Ben slipped the pipe deep into a pocket of his chaps. He wouldn't let anyone know he had found it. Or that Danger had. Not even Ann. For once he was glad that Danger couldn't quite talk!

CHAPTER THREE

The Bar-B Outfit

BEN GOT on Pilot again. Followed by Danger, he rode away from the river's edge and toward the highway. His hands were resting on the saddle horn. His head was bent and he no longer held his shoulders straight. Under his wide hatbrim, Ben's face was troubled. He was trying to remember what man he had seen lately smoking a pipe. Fred didn't. His father didn't. Who, then? And if he did think of someone, what would that mean? Hundreds of men smoked pipes. Still, Ben had the strange feeling that when he found the man who belonged to this pipe, he would know who had done the killing last night.

They came to the highway. Pie, not getting any signal from his rider, turned toward home. But Ben was too busy with his thoughts at just that minute to see that Pie had not taken the right turn. It was when Pilot, still without any signal, broke into a trot that Ben at last raised his head. When he saw the ranch house in front of him and understood what had happened, he said something under his breath. Then he pulled up and turned Pie sharply just by holding one knee tight against the pony's side.

"Think you are pretty clever, don't you?" Ben said to his horse.

Pie threw up his head as if to answer, "Better not go to sleep when you are riding me, or anything may happen. How was I to know you wanted me to go farther down the highway?"

Ben laughed and reached down to pat Pie's silky

neck. Pie's ears moved at Ben's touch. No hard feelings now!

Before long they came in sight of the Bar-B ranch buildings. As he rode toward the ranch gate, Ben saw another man on horseback coming toward him. It was Fred. Ben opened the gate and waited beside it for Fred. He saw Ben and lifted his horse into a trot.

"Hi," said Ben when the other man was close enough to hear him.

"Hi yourself," Fred called back.

Fred had come to River Ranch about a month ago. Before that, Red Casey had been riding for River Ranch. Fred was all the help that Ben and his father had, except for Juan, who was part Indian and lived with his wife on a little patch of ground up in the hills. Red Casey had been with the ranch for as far back as Ben could remember. But Red had left them to buy a ranch of his own in another part of the valley. So Fred had come in his place.

Fred was a tall, skinny fellow who never said much. Ben had found it a little hard to get to know him. But he was always friendly, and as cowhands are not given to much talk, Ben had not thought anything of it. Ben even liked Fred. The man was a good hand with horses and cattle and was not afraid of work. Ben and his father had thought that in time they might come to like him as well as they did Red. But it would take many years before Fred held the place in their hearts that Red had. Red was like one of the family.

"Find out anything?" asked Ben.

Fred shook his head. "They don't know anything," he answered.

"Did you ask them about the pickup truck?"

Fred brushed a fly off his horse's neck. "Seems like they got to use theirs today to go into town. They'll let you have it tonight, though."

"That will help a little," Ben said. His face was troubled.

One thing that had made it easy for the cattle thieves last night was that the River Ranch pickup truck had broken down. Ben had wanted to use it to patrol the highway near the ranch. But when he had gone out to start it, he had found that the battery was dead. Until he got it fixed, the truck was of no use to him. It would have to happen this way, Ben had thought, just when his father had gone off in the family car. Well, perhaps the Bar-B people would bring him out a battery from town. He'd ride in and ask them.

Ben said as much to Fred.

"Sure," Fred said, "they can do that. I thought of asking them, and then I decided I'd better let you. After all, this is your show."

He smiled across his saddle horn at Ben, and his smile held a special meaning. Ben could feel his face getting red under that smile. For three nights now, he was thinking, he had lost his father's cattle and he was no nearer now to catching the people who had taken them than on the first night. No wonder Fred was making fun of him. Even if he was older than Ben, Ben was the owner's son, and, as such, should be more on his toes than he had been so far. Why, even the pickup truck would not run! Things were in a fine way, for sure!

"Don't take it so hard," Fred said kindly. It was as if he could read Ben's mind. "Things like this can happen to any rancher now and then. And it takes a little while to get them straightened out again. If you ask me, I don't think you can do much with a truck anyway."

"Well, they seem to be doing all right," returned Ben in a sharp voice. "They don't need horses to get where they want to go. I guess if they can get around in a truck, so can I."

Fred tipped back his big hat until it rested on the very back of his head. Then he lifted his shoulders high and let them drop.

"Well, all I got to say is," he said slowly, "they sure are giving you the run-around now."

"Me?" said Ben. " I don't see that you are getting so very far with all this yourself."

"That's right," said Fred. "They got me stopped."

"Well, they haven't got me stopped yet," said

Ben, moving Pilot over toward the gate. "I'm not going to stop until I have found out who is taking our cattle."

Again Fred smiled at him. Perhaps the man was amused at the boy's helpless anger. He turned his horse and started down the highway. "Happy hunting!" he called back over his shoulder.

Ben watched him ride away. Just at that minute he didn't know quite what to make of Fred. He was part of the River Ranch outfit, but he wasn't talking like it. What had Ben done or said to make Fred suddenly start talking as if he thought Ben was a flat tire? that young man asked himself. Well, wasn't he a flat tire? He must look pretty silly to a fellow like Fred. Maybe he had taken too much upon himself. Maybe he should have gone to Fred at the beginning and let him take the lead in this business. An old cowhand might find it unpleasant having a young cub always telling him what to do. Ben guessed he had been pretty full of himself. Maybe he had been pushing Fred around a little too much. He had not meant to. Ben was not the kind to push anyone around. Except maybe Ann. And she expected it. Ben decided to ask for Fred's help a little more in the days ahead. Perhaps that would make Fred a little easier to get along with.

Ben and Pie and Danger trotted on down the little road that led to the Bar-B house. A dog rose from the dirty back steps and came toward them, growling. Danger growled a warning right back at him, and the Bar-B dog stopped in his tracks. A hungry looking cat shot under the house, where she stared out at the visitors with frightened eyes. A few chickens scratched in the dust near the back steps of the tumble-down house. And off toward the tumble-down barn a windmill squeaked as the morning breeze turned it slowly.

Ben looked about him for a minute before getting off his horse. In his mind's eye he saw the neat buildings, the straight fences, and the gay flower gardens of River Ranch. This place could do very well with some of the same kind of care his home place had. It badly needed cleaning up. Everything about the Bar-B outfit looked run down. Everything except the pickup truck. It was standing near the steps and it looked very businesslike and ready for use at any minute. Just now Ben would gladly have swapped his mother's brightest flower garden for it. Yes, at this minute Ben would have given all the flower gardens at River Ranch to have that truck.

He had wanted to use his truck today to visit the other ranchers of the valley. He wanted to tell them about the cattle killings at River Ranch and ask them to help him catch the thieves. But as there was no telephone line out this way, he would have to have a car to get around in. Now he would have to lose a day before he could start driving from ranch to ranch, rounding up help. He was sure Hank would not mind picking up a battery for him in town. Tomorrow, Ben told himself, he would be able to start doing what should be done today.

When Ben had reached this point in his thinking, the back door of the house was kicked open and a man came out. When he saw Ben he said, "Seems like all the River Ranch outfit is heading this way. Fred just left."

"Yes," said Ben, swinging off Pie, "I just met him down at your gate."

The man was Hank Horton, owner of the Bar-B. He was almost old enough to be Ben's grandfather. His hair was a dirty gray, and so were the whiskers that covered his face. He had few teeth left, and when he talked he had a bad time with his s's. He was something of a clown, was Hank Horton, and now, even in the face of all his trouble, Ben smiled just looking at him.

"Where is Andy, Hank?" Ben asked.

"Left for the hills a while back," said Hank.

Ben was suddenly interested; he didn't know exactly why. "What is he doing up there?"

"Nothing, so far as I know. Except throwing a shadow. That's about as much as Andy ever does. But nobody ever done harm to nobody throwing shadows."

He looked at Ben as if he dared him to think differently. But Ben only smiled at the bright old eyes peering into his.

Andy was Hank's twin brother and looked exactly like him, only Andy had more teeth than Hank. He was different in another way, too. Andy never talked. He listened. And sometimes he had been seen to shake his head. But he never talked. Some people said he couldn't talk. Some people thought he was not quite right in the head. But Hank always stood up for Andy against anyone. He said Andy had forgotten more than most people knew.

Ben had known the brothers half his life. He didn't understand them and he didn't very much like them. But they were harmless and, in a way, good neighbors. They always minded their own business and they never borrowed from anyone. It was for this reason that Ben didn't like asking them to do anything for him now. It was the reason Fred had left the dirty work for Ben to do. The Hortons were a queer pair, and most people let them alone.

It was not quite clear just how they made a living. They ran a few cattle themselves, and sometimes they let other ranchers' cattle feed on their grassland and made a little money that way. However, their needs were small and their costs were few. Anyone looking at their ranch and its buildings could understand easily how they could get along without working very hard. The Horton brothers didn't like work even a little bit.

"I rode over to ask you to do something for me, Hank," Ben began.

Hank's eyes looked away from him. "Don't know as I got the time just now," he cut in before Ben could finish saying what was on his mind.

Ben smiled. "I wasn't going to ask you to do any *work* for me, Hank. I just wanted you to pick up something for me in town."

"Oh-h-h," said Hank, "that's different. What you want?"

But what Ben wanted had to wait until Hank had chased away two hens who had suddenly decided to hop onto the back steps. "Scat!" he yelled at the top of his voice. His missing teeth made it sound like angry baby talk. "Scat!" He kicked at them and waved his arms. The poor hens, frightened silly, fell off the steps into the dust. The cat, unhappy at the sudden goings on, slid from beneath the house and raced for the greater safety of the barn.

"Man can't live nohow with all them animals trying to move in with him," Hank said when things had quieted down a bit. "I was telling Andy only yesterday there wasn't a bit of use trying to clean up around here so long as the animals got free way over everything."

Ben laughed. "What did Andy say?"

Hank looked sharply at him. "Don't you be getting too full of yourself, young fellow. You know as well as I do, Andy don't never say anything. That's where he's wise, too. Can't fight with a man without he talks. Right?"

"Right," Ben answered. "About that business in town," he began again.

"What about it?" asked Hank, and this time he got settled to listen.

"I need a new battery for our pickup truck. Will you get one for me?"

"You got the money to pay for it?"

"Why, yes," answered Ben, surprised at Hank's question. Did the old scarecrow think he was supposed to pay for it? Ben wondered. "I wouldn't expect you to pay for it, Hank," Ben told him. "I'll give you the money right now."

Hank took the two greenbacks Ben handed him and stuffed them into his shirt pocket. "Fred tells me you been missing some cattle."

"Yes," said Ben. "We might have caught the thieves last night if the truck had been in working order."

"Too bad," said Hank. "Makes me glad right now we don't have any good cattle to lose. Just a few skinny things, no use to nobody. Got to build our herd up one of these days." Ben smiled to himself at Hank's words. The Hortons were always going to "build up" their herd. "Well, what you don't have you can't lose," said Hank happily. "Right?"

Ben laughed. "Right," he answered. But in his heart he thought it was a very funny way to keep out of trouble.

"How about you going into town with me?" asked Hank. "Glad to have you go along and help pay for the gasoline."

"Thanks," said Ben. "Take my share of the gasoline out of the money I gave you. But I think I had better stick around here. I can't do any good in town."

"Suit yourself. I'll be starting right soon now," Hank said.

"I'll not keep you any longer then, Hank."

They said good-by to each other, and Ben got on Pilot. He whistled to Danger, who had by this time made friends with the Bar-B dog. Together they were trying to dig a rat out from under the house. Danger left his digging, but he kept looking back to where the Bar-B dog was throwing dirt in all directions.

"I'll drop the battery by," Hank promised as Ben started to ride away.

"Many thanks, Hank," Ben called back to him. He settled into the saddle and, with Danger following along behind, started Pilot across the Bar-B yard in the direction of the hills.

CHAPTER FOUR

Juan's Rancho

HANK sure is a queer old chap, Ben was thinking as the hills drew closer. Queer as a three-dollar bill.

He smiled to himself as he saw again in his mind's eye Hank's sudden way with chickens. "I must remember to tell Ann about that," he said to himself. "She'll get a big kick out of it."

The grass upon the hills was brown and dry. A few small trees made round spots of shade on it. Here and there some Bar-B cattle lay in the shade. They looked like everything else that had anything to do with that outfit. They were a mixed-up herd. There was not one really good animal among them all. Hank was quite right; they were not worth taking.

Ben thought of the good River Ranch herds. He thought of their fat and silky red sides, their white faces, their strong short horns. Their backs were straight, their legs short and stocky. Every inch of them was good meat. They were nothing like these poor, seedy-looking things. It was silly not to keep your herds pure, Ben told himself. Good cattle took no more care than poor cattle.

Then another thought came to him. Keep your heads pure and lose your cattle! No one would want to take any of the Horton cows. They were safe!

But still Ben was glad that his father's cattle were nothing like those the Horton brothers owned. A fellow could not feel proud of these. Ben knew there could be no fun in ranching if you could not feel proud of everything you owned. He was proud of River Ranch, all right. Some day, he promised himself, he was going to own a ranch just like it. But first he must catch the cattle thieves, or he would not think he was fit to own anything. A good rancher must know how to run a ranch. And letting cattle thieves kill your cows whenever they felt like it was no way to run one.

He suddenly remembered the pipe in the pocket of his chaps. He drew it out now and looked at it again. It was a good pipe. The only mark on it was where its owner had held it in his teeth. Ben gave a short laugh and put the pipe back. That let Hank out, then, as a possible cattle thief. Hank had no teeth with which to hold a pipe in his mouth.

But why had he thought of Hank along with the killings? Ben asked himself. Hank had been living next door to River Ranch for years. If he had wanted to take his neighbors' cattle, he would have started doing so long ago. Little as he cared for Hank, Ben was glad that Hank could not possibly be the thief. It was not good to think bad things of your neighbors.

As he rode along, Ben had picked up the trail leading to Juan's little place among the hills. It was the short cut. The road there was twice as long as the back trail. The trail was going up fairly straight now, and Pilot had to dig his toes in to make the climb. There was no sound except the heavy breathing of the horse, the squeak of the saddle, and the warm and sleepy noise of insects in the brush along the trail. The sun stood almost directly overhead. Danger's tongue was hanging far out of his mouth. Under the saddle blanket, Pilot's hide was wet.

The horse's hoofs made a clop-clopping sound as

he crossed a little wooden bridge over a mountain stream. In another minute, Ben was riding into Juan's dooryard.

There were two men in the dooryard. One man was sitting on the back step. The other was sitting on an old straight chair tipped back against a tree. His arms were folded, and his eyes were fastened on the ground before him. The man on the doorstep rose as Ben rode in. His smile was warm. But the other man, who was Andy Horton, went on looking at the ground as if he had not heard Pilot's thudding steps upon the hard-packed dirt of the dooryard.

"Hi, Juan," called Ben warmly to the man who had got up to meet him.

"*Buenos dias,* Ben," said Juan slowly. "It is good to see you."

He turned toward the house. "Carmela," he called, "Ben is here. He will be hungry."

An answering cry came from inside. At once the back door shot open, and a fat jolly woman hurried from the house.

"Ben, Ben," she cried. "It is good to see you. Where is Ann?"

Ben had got off Pilot by this time and was loosening the saddle. He left off to speak to Carmela.

"Ann does not even know I'm here, Carmela," he said. "She'll be pretty mad when she finds out I came without her."

"And I am already pretty mad that you do not bring her," said Carmela, her black eyes flashing. "It is two weeks now I have not seen her."

"Dad and Mom are away," Ben said, "and she is busy at the ranch."

Carmela made a round O of her mouth and bobbed her head in understanding. "I see," she said at last. "It makes everything clear. I must go down this day to help her." She turned at once to her husband. "Juan, you hear? Ann is alone with Ben at the ranch and needs me. I go to her at once."

Ben laughed. "Not so fast, Carmela. Juan may need you more than Ann does. She is getting along all right. I didn't come up here to take you away from your own home. I came to see Juan about another matter."

But Carmela was not listening to Ben as she walked quickly back toward the house. "Men do not understand these things," she was saying, more to herself than to the three men within hearing of her. "The child needs me. I go at once."

Ben let her go off chattering to herself. He knew very well from times past that there was no changing Carmela once she got an idea into her head. Before night came, Ann would have help in the house. It would matter very little to Carmela whether Ann liked it or didn't. Perhaps it would be just as well, Ben decided, thinking of the way things were. He had not liked riding off and leaving Ann alone last night.

"Hello, Andy," Ben said as he walked past the other Horton brother to take a seat beside Juan on the back step. "I just came from your place. Talked a bit with Hank. He's going to pick up a battery for me in town."

Andy looked at Ben, smiled a silly smile, and looked back at the ground again.

"What's new, Ben?" Juan asked.

"River Ranch is losing cattle, Juan," Ben answered. "Thought I'd ride up and talk it over with you."

Juan looked sharply at him. "What you mean, losing cattle? They run off? They die? What you mean?"

"I mean someone is killing them and taking the meat away to sell somewhere. Like in the old days, Juan. Cattle thieves. *Sabe?*"

"*Si,*" Juan answered softly, his face filled with surprise. "*Si.* This is bad. How many you lose?"

"Seven head."

Juan whistled low. "This is bad," he said again.

"I'll say it is," said Ben. He then told Juan of the killings. He went carefully over every bit of the story. Juan listened quietly, wagging his head now and then, his dark eyes worried. Andy, Ben saw, was listening too. But Ben cared little about him. Andy was a kind of fool, and what Ben needed right now was someone with a good head on his shoulders. Like Juan.

As far back as Ben could remember, there had been Juan and Carmela. Carmela had often helped his mother in the house. The two of them had lived for several years on River Ranch. Then Juan had decided to take up a little home place of his own. He had come up here to this out-of-the-way spot because he could live very cheaply and be free. He kept a few goats, a few chickens, and a pair of hunting dogs. He also had an old horse and an even older cart. In this he and Carmela sometimes came down to visit at River Ranch. If they ever needed to go to town, they were always sure they could catch a ride at the ranch, if not one day, then the next. Time was not important to Juan and Carmela. They did not work for or against time. Instead, they made time work for them. They were among the happiest people Ben and Ann knew. And Juan's rancho, as the young people had long called the little home among the hills, was one of their favorite visiting places. Carmela's *tamales* and *frijoles* were "out of this world," as Ann put it. Even now, the good smell of hot corn paste and tomato sauce was being carried to Ben's nose on a breeze from the kitchen. It made him remember that breakfast was now a long time behind him.

In a few minutes Carmela came to the door. "Where you eat lunch," she asked, "outside or in?"

Ben turned his head around to look up at her. "Here, thank you, Carmela," he said. "If I go inside, you'll put on a clean tablecloth and make yourself more work."

Carmela smiled down at him, and her kind face broke into deep lines that were like tiny valleys in her fat cheeks. "Okay," she said. "How about you two—*tamales?*" she asked, looking angrily from her husband to Andy and back to Juan again. But she was not angry. It was just Carmela's way to look angry like that.

Andy bobbed his head and smiled his silly smile. Juan said, "*Si,* Carmela."

Soon the three men were hungrily eating Carmela's good food. A little way off from them, Juan's dogs and Danger watched interestedly. Now and then they licked their lips as if trying to get it across to their masters that they could do with a bite too. But the men did not even look at them. After a while the dogs gave up and lay down. But they never took their eyes off the three who were eating.

At last, their lunch finished, Carmela came out and gathered up the plates and forks. Then she said, "Now I wash the dishes. Then I shall put on a clean dress. And then Juan shall drive me down to the ranch."

"Okay, Carmela," said Juan quietly. He too knew it was no use trying to change Carmela's mind. Also, he was thinking that it might not be a bad idea for him to be around if Ben were in trouble. Ben was like a son to Juan.

The noise of Carmela's dishwashing was like a background to the rest of Ben's talk with Juan. Most of the time Andy sat upon the chair tipped back against the tree. For a while he stretched out upon the ground and seemed to sleep. When at last Ben had told Juan all he knew, and they had talked it over until there was nothing left to say about it, Andy went away. He didn't say a word. He just walked out of the dooryard and over the bridge and out of sight.

"He's sure a queer one, isn't he?" Ben said to Juan.

The old man lifted his shoulders. "I do not know why he come here," he said. "All at once, I look up and here he is. He smile; I smile back. I talk; he listen. He say nothing."

"Does he come here often?" Ben asked.

Juan shook his head. "Almost I would say never. Some time," he tipped his head back and stared at the sky for a minute, "maybe a month back, he come here. Then we smoke and sit like today. But he say nothing. Nothing at all."

Ben's head began to spin. "You say he was smoking when he was here before?"

Juan moved his head up and down slowly and looked wonderingly at his young visitor.

"But he wasn't smoking today!"

Juan's shoulders lifted again in the easy way he had. "That is right. But it is not strange," Juan said. "One day a man smokes; another day he does not. So what?"

"What was he smoking?"

"A pipe. What else?"

"Why do you say 'what else'?" Ben asked.

"Have you never seen?" Juan asked. "Andy never smoke anything except a pipe. But Ben, why all this over a man and a pipe? You talk like little child. What is so strange about this thing?"

Ben tried to make up his mind. Should he tell Juan about the pipe he had found, or should he not? He had promised himself never to tell anyone about it, and yet, if Juan should say for sure that it was Andy's, it might clear up the whole thing. And again, it might clear up nothing at all. Should he tell?

He looked into Juan's black eyes, now looking

into his. The older man was waiting for an answer. Should Ben put him off, or tell him everything?

Suddenly Ben made up his mind. He had known Juan all his life. Juan had always been faithful. It was foolish, Ben thought, not to tell him. The pipe was, so far, the only thing they had to go on in trying to find the cattle thieves. Juan would just about have to know about it. Ben reached into the pocket of his chaps. He drew out the pipe and held it out to Juan.

"At the place where the cattle were killed last night I found this pipe, Juan. Could you tell me who might have lost it? I thought perhaps one of the thieves might have dropped it . . ."

Juan was reaching out his hand for the pipe. He picked it up and looked it over carefully. Then he looked from the pipe straight into Ben's eyes.

"But yes," he said in a voice which was not afraid. "I know this pipe very well. It is the one Carmela gave to me last Christmas. Thank you, Ben. I am very glad to have it back."

CHAPTER FIVE

Carmela Speaks Out

BEN HAD time for much thinking on the way home. Juan and Carmela rode ahead of him in the old cart. Its seat dipped sharply on Carmela's side as the springs were squashed almost flat by her weight. Juan would have slid down the seat if her wide body had not kept him pushed to his own side. The old horse went slowly, and the cart wheels squeaked loudly as they bumped over the dirt road. Pilot threw up his head and made it clear that he did not like following these people. Juan's two dogs trotted just under the back part of the cart. Danger trotted just behind Pilot.

It took nearly half the afternoon to get to River Ranch. By the time they arrived there Ben was no closer to finding out who the cattle thieves were than when he had first started out this morning. The matter of Juan's pipe had only made things harder. What was it doing there where the killings had taken place? Juan had said that he had not been at that spot beside the river, and Ben had believed him. How, then, had the pipe got there? Could Juan be lying? It was foolish even to think so, let alone to believe such a thing, Ben told himself. But how had the pipe got there?

Ann was delighted to see Carmela. They threw their arms around each other in a huge hug. As Ben watched their meeting, he thought that perhaps Ann had been lonely, and he was sorry that he had not thought of getting Carmela before now. It would be good to know that Ann was not alone in the house when he rode out tonight. For Ben was sure he would be out tonight. He only hoped that Hank would bring the battery back so that he could use the truck.

"Has Hank come back yet?" Ben asked Ann. "He was going to bring us a battery from town."

She shook her head. "Not yet," she said.

"Where's Fred?" Ben wanted to know.

"He rode up toward Pine Flat to mend fence," Ann answered.

Ben remembered. A few cattle had broken through at that place yesterday. It was a funny thing the way the grass always looked greener to a cow on the other side of the fence. They could stand in grass to their shoulders, then break down a fence to get at some dried-up milkweed they didn't want after they got there. Mending fence was a never-ending job on a cattle ranch.

Ann settled Juan and Carmela in their room; then Juan joined Ben, and the two men were soon busy with the many things that needed doing. Ann and Carmela were just as busy inside the house. Ann had got behind with the ironing. It didn't take long for Carmela's eagle eyes to find this out. Soon the thumping of the flatiron could be heard from the kitchen. Ann brought her basket of mending, and the two womenfolk visited while they did their work.

It was good to have Carmela here, Ann was thinking. She had missed her mother more and more as the days passed. This trouble with the cattle thieves had made her jumpy, too. She was glad of the older woman's company. She hoped Carmela would stay until Dad and Mom got back.

As if in answer to this hope, Carmela looked up from the ironing board. "When your mother come back?" she asked in the short way of speaking she had.

"We don't know for sure," Ann said.

"You must know something," Carmela told her as she folded a tablecloth and banged the iron down upon it. "Is she come tomorrow? Or does she come for Christmas?"

Ann laughed. "I don't look for her tomorrow. And she had better not stay away until Christmas!" Then she added, "We think they will be gone for several more days. They expected to be gone about ten days when they left. We have had one letter from them. They seem to be having a fine time."

"Good," said Carmela. Her wide back was turned to Ann as she dug into the basket of clothes for another piece to iron. "But if they come tomorrow or next year, I stay until they come. It is no good to have little girl stay all alone in big house."

Ann looked cross, but she said, "I am glad you want to stay, Carmela. Thank you. But I am not a little girl any longer. I am fifteen. And also I am not alone here. Ben is with me, don't forget."

"Ben not with you last night. Ben gone most of today. What you mean, Ben is with you?"

"Well, he was only gone part of the night. And Fred has been on the place all day. You are just frightening yourself, Carmela."

All Carmela said in return to this was one word.

"Fred!" she snorted. But the way in which she spoke the man's name made Ann look up quickly.

Carmela's kindly face was black as a storm cloud. She banged the iron over the towel she was working on as if she were angry at it.

"Why, Carmela!" said Ann, surprised. "You sound as if you didn't like Fred."

"That is right," returned Carmela. "Him I do not like."

"But why? Fred is a good hand. What has he ever done to you or Juan?"

"He has done nothing. But still I do not like him. Always he stands and looks and says little. I do not like the feel of his eyes upon me. It is as if they said, 'She is fat.' I do not like people that make me feel my fat."

Ann laughed until tears filled her eyes. She had to lay down her needle and wipe her eyes on the shirt she was mending. Still laughing, she spoke to Carmela.

"Aren't you ashamed of yourself not to like a

person for the thoughts you put into his head yourself! That is not fair, Carmela, and you know it. And then, there is no getting around it—you *are* fat, you know. And you don't need to be," Ann hurried on as Carmela's angry eyes flashed up at her. "If you just didn't eat quite so many *tamales* and *frijoles* you'd soon be as thin as a deer."

"All right," said Carmela. "So it is my fault that I am fat. But just the same, I do not like that Fred of yours. He makes me feel uncomfortable. I do not like such people."

"Well, try and get along with him while you are here, please, Carmela. Good hands are not easy to come by. And Fred *is* a good hand. We like him all right."

Carmela snorted again at this but said no more, and they began talking of other things.

It was late in the afternoon when Hank Horton drove in with the battery. Ben and Juan were at the barn putting up hay. They left their job as the pickup truck came rattling into the ranch yard.

"Well, there she is," said Hank, pointing to the square box on the floor of the truck. He made no move to help Ben lift it out. But Ben had not expected any help.

"Thanks for bringing it to me, Hank. Let me know any time I can do something for you," Ben said.

"Glad to help out a neighbor," said Hank, just as if he really meant it. From far under the overhanging brush of his eyebrows, his beady little eyes shone sharply. Looking at him, Ben thought that there wasn't much of Hank's face that showed. Just a patch of lined skin between his eyebrows and his whiskers. "Here's your change," said Hank.

Ben put down the heavy box and held out his hand. Hank placed some money in it, counting it out carefully.

"And here is the bill for the battery, all marked right as rain."

Ben looked at the bill and at the change in his hand. As Hank had said, it was all as right as rain.

Then Ben picked up the battery, and Hank jumped back into his truck and roared away.

Ben looked over his shoulder at the truck rocking out of the yard. "So help me," he said to Juan as he started for his own truck, "I sometimes think that if Hank had a propeller on the front of that thing, it would take off and zoom into the wild blue—"

He didn't finish, for just then the slippery box slid out of his hands and nearly fell to the ground.

"Ought to make these so a fellow can carry them," Ben growled, taking a tighter hold on the box.

Supper was early that night, for Ben wanted to start out as soon as possible after the new battery was put into the truck. The pickup was ready now, and working beautifully. Ben expected to drive a good part of the night. He wanted to visit as many of the neighboring ranches as he could. There was no time to lose in getting the Prairie Patrol together. Already Ben was thinking of it by that name. He didn't know just how it would work, or what it would do; but in his own mind it already had a name. While

River Ranch could hardly be said to be a prairie ranch, still the flat land within this valley was not unlike a prairie. And Ben liked the sound of the two words together: Prairie Patrol. They had an important kind of ring. They sounded like a bunch of men who could get things done. They sounded like the old West.

It was planned that while he was gone Juan and Fred would watch the ranch. Ben was well pleased with the way things were going along.

But they didn't go quite so well when supper was over. It was then that Ann took a hand in them.

Ann pushed her chair away from the table the same minute Ben did. "I'll get my things," she told him. "I won't be a minute."

Ben drew himself up as tall as he could get, which was something over six feet. He looked down crossly as his sister. "May I ask just what you are planning to do?" he said.

"Oh, that's right," said Ann. "I guess I forgot to tell you. I'm going with you tonight."

"You *thought* you were going with me," Ben said, looking meaner by the minute.

"It's no use, Ben. I don't frighten easily. Anyway, not by you. So stop looking so mean. I have decided I am going, and that is all there is to it."

"Ann—" Ben began, but Ann stopped him.

"Now look, Ben. There is no reason in the world why I shouldn't go along with you tonight. You are going to see a good many people that I would like to see too. I've been stuck here for days now, and it's not fair to make me stay behind when there is no good reason for my staying. You know there will be no danger in what you are going to do tonight. And I would love the ride. Please?"

Ben looked at her a long minute. Ann's eyes never left his face. They were blacker than ever, with her longing to go showing deep inside them. He smiled a little.

"Oh, all right," he said. "But I am warning you right now. We may be out all night."

"Oh, goody," cried Ann. "I've always wanted to stay out all night. Won't Mom be surprised when she hears about it!"

But Ben just looked more unhappy than ever and made no answer.

CHAPTER SIX

Prairie Patrol

IT WAS a beautiful night. The mountains stood up dark against the star-filled sky. Ann took a deep breath and tipped her head back against the seat of the pickup truck. An owl floated across the road in front of them.

"There goes some bad news for any ground squirrel who has not found his hole yet," said Ben as the owl floated past. Soon his shadowy body was lost in the deeper shadow of the night.

Her brother's words troubled Ann. It was too fine a night to think of such unpleasant things. She said so to Ben. But he only laughed. "It is the way of this world," he told her. "If some things were not killed, other things could not live."

"I don't like to think of anything being killed on such a night as this. I've come along to have a good time," she said.

"Okay, Sis, have a good time," her brother returned pleasantly. "But what I'm thinking about is not exactly fun. And it has to do with killing."

She looked over at him quickly. "Ben, what do you mean?"

He patted her hand. "Not what you think, Ann. The only killings in this thing will be cattle killings."

"But what will you do when you catch the thieves? Suppose they decide to shoot it out with you?"

"The first answer is easy," Ben said. "We'll put them away where they can't make any more trouble. The second part of what you just asked is not so easy to answer, however. But I suppose, if they want to shoot it out with us, we will give them what they ask for."

Ann looked worried. "Then there may be shooting after all?" she said.

"There may be shooting after all," Ben answered. "But we hope not, and we shall do all we can to keep it from happening. That is why I am going out to-night to talk to the ranchers round about. Perhaps when the bad men learn that the whole country is wise to what they are doing, they will know the game is up. It is the only way I can see to stop them. If the ranchers are willing to help me catch the thieves, then we will all go to town and have the head of the police there make us policemen too, with the right to patrol the countryside."

"Couldn't the policemen in town take over the job?" asked Ann. She didn't like the idea of her brother being a country copper.

"No," said Ben very decidely. "There would not be nearly enough policemen for the job. When a thing like this comes up, the ranchers must get together and fight their own war. But they must do it as an orderly body and not as a bunch of hard-boiled, half-baked simpletons having a good time on a man hunt. We will have a leader and patrol the countryside. Each man will know just what to do and when. And at all times the head of the police in town will know what we are doing."

Ann said nothing to this, and Ben added, "You just wait and see. In no time at all after the Prairie Patrol goes to work the trouble will be over."

With this comforting thought, Ann turned her face to the stars again.

Ben had told Ann of one reason why he wanted to talk to his neighbors tonight. But the other reason he had not told her. He wanted, also, to know if any of them had been losing cattle too. It would make quite a bit of difference in Ben's thinking if the killings had happened only to River Ranch cattle. It might mean that the killers were closer to that part of the valley than to any other. And it might mean that they were from town and stopped at River Ranch because it happened to be the first really large cattle ranch they came to. But if a rancher ten or fifteen miles away had also been losing cattle, then it would be clear that the thieves were striking in all parts of the valley; and they might be coming from all parts of the valley too.

They rode for about three miles before they came to a high ranch gate. Ann jumped down from the truck to open it. Ben drove through, while Ann held the gate and shut her eyes against the brightness of the headlights. Then Ben stopped while Ann fastened the gate. In the stillness the waiting truck chugged like a tired animal short of breath. In a few seconds Ann was climbing back into her seat again. This was the old Quito Ranch and was owned by a big, goodhearted man named Percival Smith. Everyone called him "Windy," however. It suited him much better than did "Percival." A great talker, Windy.

"You will be lucky if you get a chance to make any other calls tonight," Ann said as the truck bumped over the road toward the lights of the ranch house.

"I'll make it as short as I can," Ben said, knowing it would not be easy.

The Smiths were glad to see their young neighbors. While Ben talked to Windy on the back porch, Ann helped the oldest Smith girl with the supper dishes, while Mrs. Smith put the baby to bed.

For once Windy had little to say as Ben told him of what had been happening at River Ranch. He only whistled when Ben told how many cattle he had lost, and kept his eyes fixed on Ben's face.

He answered, "No," when Ben asked him if he had lost any cows. Then Windy seemed to find his tongue at last. "But I will," he said. "Just you wait. I'll be next in line. They won't overlook me. Why should they? My cows are as good as yours. Where did you say your father was? Oh yes, you don't know for sure. Well, send for him. Oh yes, that's right. He is traveling and you can't get hold of him. Well, that makes it bad. But you can count on me. I'll be right in there pitching every minute." There followed a long string of words that the cattle thieves would not have been very happy to hear. At last Ben was able to get a word in.

"I am going to try to get over to see Red Casey before I get home tonight," he said.

"Why, man," Windy began, "that's a good thirty miles. You can't do that and see all the ranchers along the way. But Red is a mighty good man. A mighty good man."

"Red is the best, Windy. I had thought of asking him to be the leader of our patrol. Would you be willing to follow him?"

"Willing?" roared Windy. "I'd follow him walking on my hands through a cactus patch. Like I say, you can count on me."

Ben smiled. "Believe me, Windy, I know that."

"By the way," said Windy as Ben started to edge away from him. "How about the Horton boys? Talked to them yet?"

"Yes. I talked to them this morning. Or, to be more nearly right, I talked to Hank."

Windy wagged his head. "That Andy," he said,

touching his forehead. "He's not quite all there."

"It's pretty hard to tell about that unless a man says something once in a while," said Ben. "Sometimes I think Andy is plenty smart. Too smart to let on he knows anything."

Windy rubbed a big hand slowly along his jaw and eyed Ben. "Say-y-y," he said, drawing out the word, "you know you might have something there. I knew a fellow once . . ."

Ben looked toward the kitchen door. The two men were standing on the back porch just outside the patch of light coming through the open kitchen door. Ben knew he was caught. Windy had started one of his long-winded stories. If only Ann would come out and break it off, Ben was thinking. As if he had spoken his thought, she was suddenly standing framed in the open door. The light from the kitchen shining behind her made her body a slender shadow without face or color.

"Ben, if you stay to visit any longer, we'll never get through tonight," she said.

"That's right," Ben said quickly. "Well, so long, Windy. I'll keep in touch with you. Mighty good of you to help."

He held out his hand, and Windy, still going on about the fellow he once knew, took Ben's hand and shook it hard. Then, still talking, he followed them to the truck. He was still talking when they drove, waving, out of the yard.

"Glad I took you along after all, Sis." Ben laughed.

"Well, that's mighty nice of you," Ann returned, and Ben laughed harder at the way she said it.

The other stops were shorter. It was only a little past one o'clock when they drove into Red Casey's dooryard. The little house was dark, but a dog came barking toward the pickup. In a minute a light came on in Red's bedroom, and a voice roared out the open window, "Who is it?"

"It's me, Red. I mean it's us, Ann and Ben."

"Be right with you. Come on in."

They went in. Ben lit the coal-oil lamp on the

table, and Ann looked around Red's kitchen. It was a sorry sight. Without waiting for the master of the house, she began drawing water in the teakettle. She set it on the oil stove and lighted the burner under it.

"There won't be time for that," said Ben.

"Oh, yes there will," Ann told him. "I'm going to take time. We only have to drive straight home. We should be there by four o'clock at the latest. With Juan and Carmela there, we can sleep until eight."

While she talked, Ann moved about, putting away boxes of food and gathering the dirty dishes in one place. Before Red came in, the kitchen already looked as if a woman's hand had been laid upon it.

He was suddenly standing in the doorway, his red hair on end. He looked at the two before entering the room. His eyes were red, and his voice was thick with sleep.

"What's wrong?"

Ben told him, and Ann tried hard not to rattle the dishes more than she had to.

"So I've come to ask you to be leader of the Prairie Patrol," Ben finished. "Everybody's for it."

Red looked over at Ben and smiled his slow smile. "Did you dream up the name all by yourself, or did it just hit you sudden like?"

Ben's face got red. "We've got to call ourselves something," he said. "I thought that would be easy to remember."

"Sure," said Red, still smiling. "Easy, like the Pony Express. Maybe we'll write the last word to the story of the Wild West. 'And then the Prairie Patrol came riding, and the bad men bit the dust.' " He reached out and gave Ben a brotherly punch. "Sure, I'll lead your old patrol. It's a good idea, and I was only fooling. But just at first it sort of sounded a little too much like a moving pitcher."

"*Pic-ture,*" Ann said, turning from her dishwashing. "Ever since I was born I have been trying to get you to say 'picture' instead of 'pitcher.' When are you going to learn?"

" 'Ever since I was born,' " Ben snorted. "Anyone

would think you had come talking into the world."

Red laughed. "Sometimes I think she did, at that."

Ann made a face at them and returned to her work.

"Mighty nice of you to wash my dishes, Ann. I had just about got to where I had to turn them over and use the other side."

"When are you going to get married, Red, and start living a good life?" Ann asked him.

"Why, Annie, you surprise me," Red said. "Don't you remember, I'm waiting for you to grow up!"

"Oh, that's right," Ann laughed. "How could I have forgotten that?"

It was an old joke between them. Ever since Ann could remember, Red had been waiting for her to grow up and marry him. For about as long a time, she had been trying to teach him to say "picture" instead of "pitcher." There was as much chance of the one happening as the other. But they both liked the joking. Ben and Ann looked upon Red Casey as a big brother. And he thought the ground they walked over was special ground.

By the time Ben and Ann started away from Red's ranch, everything had been decided about the patrol. Fred was to take Red's place on the Casey ranch. He would go there in the pickup truck, and Red would return in it and stay at River Ranch until Ben's father came home. In the meantime, the patrol would get ready to go to work.

A gentle light was breaking above the eastern mountains when the little truck turned at last into River Ranch. A very tired young man sat at its wheel. He sat very straight because a very tired young lady had gone to sleep with her head against his shoulder.

Ben stopped beside the back porch. For a minute he looked down at his sister's sleeping face. Then he gave her a very small shake, and she opened her dark eyes and stared up at him.

"Home," he said softly. "In four hours you can help Carmela with the breakfast dishes."

Ann sat up and yawned at the dawn. "Prairie

Patrol, my eye," she said. "Prairie *Kitchen Police* would be closer to it." She yawned again. "I wonder why Red never thought of using paper plates?" she asked, climbing wearily down from the car.

"Probably afraid someone might catch him at it," said Ben. "Imagine a cowhand eating off a paper plate!"

Ann said nothing to that. She was much too sleepy to care that she had let Ben have the last word. As they entered the house, the first fingers of sunlight were feeling their way across the flat land below the mountains. It would be another warm day, Ben was thinking, as they went quietly through the sleeping house.

CHAPTER SEVEN

Hank Joins the Patrol

BEN SLEPT very little as the day spread over the valley. His head was buzzing with the plans that had been made on his visits to the neighboring ranchers. Tomorrow they would gather together at

River Ranch, and the head of the police from town would be there to change them from ranchers into real policemen. After he had spoken a few words to them, and they had raised their right hands and promised to do as he said, they would have the right to take and hold anyone they found killing cattle. They would be a real patrol. Thinking of this, Ben wished they could have come together today. But before they could do that, Red Casey would have to be there. He was to be their leader. They would do as he told them. And Red Casey could not come to River Ranch until Fred had gone up to Red's ranch to take his place there.

As soon as Ben heard Carmela moving about in the kitchen, he jumped out of bed and began getting into his jeans.

Fred, who had his bed in a room at the top of the tank house, came into the kitchen soon after Ben did. He spoke to Carmela. But she returned his "good morning" with a sharp voice and an angry look. When she set Fred's plate down in front of him, she banged it on the table so hard that the pancakes bounced on it. Fred only smiled and reached out to cut a big piece of butter from the two-pound roll of it which Carmela had set down in the middle of the table.

As soon as he had buttered his pancakes, Ben said to Fred, "Red Casey is coming over from his ranch to lead our man hunt. We decided to have you drive up to his place in the truck, and he will drive it back here. You are to stay at his ranch until such time as he decides to return to it."

Fred laid down his knife and looked at Ben. "Would you just as soon say that over again?" he asked.

Ben returned his look with some surprise. "You heard me," he told Fred. "What's the matter, don't you want to go?"

Fred put a forkful of breakfast into his mouth and chewed slowly on it for a minute before he answered Ben. At last he said, "I guess it don't matter where I work. Only I signed on to ride for River Ranch. I don't like being pushed around like that. Seems like you could have told me about what you had planned before you pulled me into it."

Ben's face slowly grew red. He knew Fred was right. No man had a right to fix things up for another without first telling him about it. He remembered what he had been thinking only yesterday morning while he was with Fred at the Horton ranch gate. He had decided that he had been pushing Fred around too much. He had thought then that Fred didn't like being pushed around. Now he had done it again, only more so. Suppose Fred should say he wouldn't go?

"I'm sorry, Fred. I didn't have anything really planned when I started out last night. It was all kind of thought up suddenly as I talked to the different ranchers. Red couldn't just leave his ranch a man short. It may only be for a few days. In the meantime, he'll take your place here."

"Casey's ranch is a good thirty miles from here, isn't it?" Fred asked.

"Yes," said Ben, his voice far from happy.

"I got to think it over," said Fred. "Seems like a lot of foolishness, all this playing at Wild West with real guns."

"How can you say that when we have already lost seven head of cattle?" said Ben. "Those cows weren't playing, you know. They were really killed. And somebody took the meat away and really sold it somewhere for real money. I don't see how you can call it play when we want to find out who really did it."

"That is just what I say," Carmela cut in before Fred had a chance to say anything. "And what is more," she went on, "it looks very queer to me that you do not want to help Ben all you can. If Red Casey is worth more at catching the cattle thieves than you, then why you don't go gladly and let him take your place?"

Her eyes flashed with anger as she fixed them on Fred and waited for his answer.

Ben was almost as angry with Carmela as she was with Fred. Now the fat would be in the fire. He had never wanted Fred to feel that his services were not so important as Red's. That wasn't the idea at all. It was just that Red knew all the cattlemen round about, and to most of them Fred was a stranger. And Ben had begun to feel that the job was too big for him. He wanted an older man, one they all believed in, to take over the job of running down the killers. Now Carmela had shot off her mouth and really made Fred mad. Everything would be just ducky now! He held his breath and waited for Fred to speak. When he did, Carmela was tongue-tied by his words.

"Come to think of it," said Fred, his voice as friendly as could be, "you may be right at that. Sure, I'll go up to Casey's. When do you want me to leave?"

For a minute Ben could hardly get his thoughts together. Fred had changed so quickly and so completely that he had taken Ben quite by surprise. But at last he was able to say, "The sooner, the better."

"Okay," said Fred. "Soon as I get my things together, I'll be off."

About thirty minutes later the pickup truck, with Fred at the wheel, drove out of the River Ranch yard. In the back of it, along with a bundle of clothes, was Fred's saddle. Ben stood and watched the truck out of sight. For some reason that he could not have told anyone, he didn't feel easy about Fred's going. Standing there and trying to decide what there was about it that troubled him, Ben felt more worried by the minute. Why had Fred suddenly decided to be pleasant about going, after the stand he had taken in the beginning? What had there been in Carmela's words to make him want to change? Ben wished he could remember more clearly just what she had said. Whatever those words were, they had made Fred decide to do as Ben wanted. Maybe he ought to turn over the running of the ranch to Carmela until Dad got back, Ben thought with a smile. Then another thought crowded that one out of his head. Boy, but he would be glad when Dad *did* get back! Things would sure straighten themselves out fast then.

Later in the morning Juan left for his own place. The animals there would need his care. He would stay up there overnight and watch the River Ranch land from that side. As he drove away in the old cart, a thin line of blue smoke trailed back over one of his shoulders. Seeing it, Ben began to wonder again, as he had so many times before, just how Juan's pipe had happened to be lying near the river's edge yesterday morning.

Red arrived early in the afternoon. Things began to look better to Ben as soon as Red drove in. He had taken time to show Fred around the place, and to break him in to some of its special needs.

"He took hold like an old hand," said Red, and added, "He is a good man. Hope you can keep him."

Ben said nothing. A few minutes later he and Red were rolling up the highway in the truck on their way into town. They were going to tell the man who was head of the town policemen about the cattle thieves and to ask him to come to River Ranch next day to make the men of the patrol into real policemen.

So the next morning, around ten o'clock, he arrived at the ranch. Soon after that the ranchers began to arrive too. In a little while the ranch yard was full of cars and small trucks. Ann and Carmela were busy in the kitchen, for it had been planned to give the men a picnic lunch under the trees at the side of the house.

A little distance from the picnic place, Ben had dug a long, deep hole. He had made a fire in the hole. Then he had placed some irons over the fire. On the irons he had laid several huge pieces of good meat. Now the meat was roasting. The good smell of the roasting meat reached the men sitting about and talking on the grass under the trees. It made them hungry. They could smell the good cooking in the kitchen too. There Carmela was making *tortillas* and cooking beans to eat with the meat. It would be a feast that they would all remember for a long time to come.

At last, when everyone had eaten all he could hold, the man from town called the ranchers together. He stood on the porch steps a few feet above them. Every man kept his eyes on the policeman. He asked them to raise their right hands. Every man did. Then the head of the police asked them if they promised to do as he told them and not to let any danger keep them from trying to catch the cattle thieves. The ranchers all promised with one voice. Then the policeman named Red Casey as their leader, and Red went and stood beside him on the steps. When they saw him the ranchers sent up a cheer at which he looked very uncomfortable, and his face got red. Ann and Ben, who were standing side by side, gave each other a little punch in the ribs and smiled toward Red. They knew how he felt, but they were happy that their friend was so well-liked by everyone.

Red told the men what he thought it was best for them to do. For the most part, they were to patrol their own ranches, and if they found any cattle killed they were to notify him at once. In the meantime, several ranchers were asked to stay at River Ranch and help patrol it, as it was the one place so far which had lost cattle.

After Red had finished talking to the men, they started back to their own ranches, while everyone left at River Ranch pitched in to help Carmela and Ann clear up after the picnic.

The last rancher had driven away from River Ranch. The picnic things were all cleared away. Red and Ben and the man from town were talking over last-minute plans. Suddenly their talk was broken up by the roar of a truck coming swiftly up the road into the ranch yard. It had no top on it; and sitting at the wheel, bent over like a race-track driver, was Hank Horton. He wore an old black hat pulled down low on his head. Under it his whiskers looked wilder than ever. He stopped the truck, and the men watching him stepped back out of the dust cloud that settled over it.

"What's been going on here?" Hank asked, without troubling to say hello. "I just seen a whole bunch of cars coming out of this place. What's going on?"

Now Ben felt as uncomfortable as Red had felt when he faced the patrol for the first time. For Ben was remembering that he had forgotten to ask the Horton brothers to join the patrol! It had never entered his head to ask them. Somehow you didn't think of the Horton brothers as ranchers. They were just a queer old pair who somehow were able to hang on to their ranch from year to year. They never seemed to be a part of the valley. But they were, and Ben was remembering it now, and feeling very unhappy as he remembered it.

Ben stepped bravely forward and looked steadily

into Hank's bright little eyes. "Do you remember my telling you the other day about the cattle that have been killed on this ranch?"

"Seems like I remember you saying something about it," said Hank.

"Well," began Ben slowly, "we have just gathered together all the ranchers around here into a patrol to catch the cattle thieves."

"That's mighty interesting," said Hank. "It's a wonder you wouldn't let an old neighbor in on your plans. Not very friendly, I calls it."

Before Ben could answer, the policeman from town stepped up to the truck. "It's not too late now. What's your name?"

"Hank Horton," said the little man, drawing himself up a bit and looking at the policeman with sharp eyes. "Lived in this valley eight years, and I'm not afraid of any man, copper or whatever."

The policeman laughed. "Well, we aren't saying that you need to be. I just thought I'd make you one of the Prairie Patrol."

"How you going to do it?" asked Hank. His eyes had a new look in them. "And who is going to tell me what to do? And what do I have to do?"

The policeman explained these things, one by one, to him. At last Hank said, "Okay. Shoot."

So the policeman asked Hank to raise his right hand. In another minute the Prairie Patrol had a new patrolman. But for some reason which he did not quite understand, Ben did not feel very happy about Hank's joining them. He was such a queer old duck. And then there was Andy. Would Andy want to join up too? he asked Hank.

"Not likely. Not likely a-tall," said Andy's brother. Then he shook a dirty finger at the three of them standing beside the truck. "But you mark my words. When the killers are found, it will be Andy who finds them. He gets around, he does. There isn't nothing goes on around here Andy don't know about."

Red and the policeman laughed at Hank's words, for they knew Andy too. The idea of his catching anyone was pretty funny. But Ben didn't laugh. There was something in what Hank had said which had started him thinking. "There isn't nothing goes on around here Andy don't know about."

I wonder, thought Ben. I wonder.

Did Andy perhaps know who the thieves were and couldn't say because he couldn't talk?

"Hank," Ben spoke sharply, "can Andy write?"

Hank shook his head. "He never went to school. Me, I got through the fourth grade and I can sign my name real good. But Andy never went. Never could make him talk. No use going to school without you can give the right words back to the teacher. And Andy didn't never have no words a-tall. He can't write nothing. Not even his name."

Ben said nothing more, but he thought, Well, that settles that. If Andy can't talk and he can't write, even if he does know who the thieves are, the secret is safe with him. But he doesn't know. It's just Hank's way of always taking Andy's part against anyone who might laugh at him. In his own funny way, I guess Hank cares quite a bit about his twin.

In another minute, Hank had turned the truck in a tight circle. Before his dust had settled he was halfway to the highway, hanging tight to the wheel, his whiskers flying.

CHAPTER EIGHT

Hands Up!

For the next three days things were quiet at River Ranch. Though Ben and Red combed every inch of ranch land, not a sign did they see of the cattle thieves. No skins were found drying in the sun. Now and then one of the big black birds that live on rotten meat was seen floating in slow circles in the blue sky. When this happened, Ben would call Danger and ride to the spot the bird shadowed. There man and dog would go carefully over the ground. But nothing more exciting than a dead rabbit or ground squirrel did they ever find.

Juan came down to the ranch with news that no cattle had been killed anywhere near him. It began to look to everyone as if the Prairie Patrol had frightened the killers away.

Then, on the fourth day following the picnic, the postman put two letters into the River Ranch mailbox. One was from Ben's mother. She and his father were having a fine time and didn't know for sure yet just when they would be home. If their children wanted to send them a letter, it would reach them in the next place they planned to visit, and she named the place. Ann sat right down to have a letter ready if anyone should stop by on the way into town.

"Shall I tell them about the cattle killings?" she asked Ben, who was placing the second letter on the chimneypiece.

Ben took a minute to think over her question. "Yes," he said at last. "We had better tell them as much as we know about it and what we have done. The news will bring them back home, and I am sorry to cut their trip short. But I think as long as we know now where to reach them, we should let Dad know what is happening."

"I think so too," said Ann.

Soon her pen was scratching busily across the paper. Suddenly she lifted her head. "What's that letter up there?"

"That one is for Red. Maybe I'd better take it to him." With that, Ben reached out, picked up the letter again, and stuck it in his shirt pocket.

Pie was waiting at the back steps when Ben went outside. He had left the pony there when he went in to give Ann the letter. Now Ben swung into the saddle and started Pie toward the pasture where some cattle were being fattened up for market. In another week they would be ready to ship. Ben knew that Red was there.

"Got something for you," shouted Ben.

Red rode over to the fence.

"Here's a letter," said Ben and handed it to him.

Red tore it open and began to read. Ben's eyes were on the cattle feeding quietly in the green pasture. He was thinking what a fine herd they were, and what a good price they would bring when they were shipped. Suddenly a sound from Red made Ben look toward him.

"Anything the matter?" asked Ben.

Red's face had gone white. "I'll say there is," he answered. "This letter is from Fred. Two head of cattle have been killed on my place."

"No!" breathed Ben. It seemed to him as if the very ground were dropping away from him. So the thieves had struck again! And in a new part of the valley! This was really bad.

"It must have happened the day after Fred got

there," Red was saying. "This letter was mailed that day. It would take a day to get here. If only we had telephones in this valley!"

"We will have when ten more ranchers come into it," said Ben. "But that won't help us much now. I'm sorry, Red. I feel that it was largely my fault for taking you away from your place."

"It's nobody's fault. It looks as if the killers were planning to work as far from River Ranch as they could. Things have got too hot for them around here."

"Yes," said Ben. "But what are you going to do, Red?"

"We'll send the men home who have been watching this place, and I'll go back to mine and keep some of the men with me there."

"Keep Fred too," said Ben. "I can get Juan to help me do whatever needs doing. Things will be pretty quiet around here until next week when we ship these cattle. Dad will be home by then. Fred and Juan and Dad and I can drive them to the railroad."

"All right, Ben. And thanks. Fred is a good man, and I think I may need him before this week is over."

So Red hurried off in the pickup truck. That night Ben and Juan took turns riding herd on the cattle in the pasture. If the killers struck at River Ranch again, Ben felt sure it would be these cattle they would choose.

The next day, when Juan returned to his own place, Carmela went with him. "It is foolish for you to stay with me," Ann had said, "when Juan needs you there to take care of the animals and the chickens while he helps Ben. Juan can't very well be in two places at once, and Ben needs him more than I need you."

So Carmela, though she liked it not at all, went with her husband. There was good reason in what Ann had said, and even Carmela could find nothing to say against it. With Carmela at Juan's rancho, Juan himself could take Fred's place at River Ranch.

Ben wondered as the day wore on just what might

be happening at Red Casey's ranch. Again he felt helpless, with the pickup truck gone. Dad ought to have Ann's letter by tomorrow. Soon he would be home. But then, anything might happen before he could get here. It was a very unhappy Ben who unsaddled Pilot at sundown and turned him loose in the corral with a friendly slap on his warm, silky neck.

The next morning Ann rose and cooked breakfast for Ben and Juan. Then she fed the chickens and washed the dishes. After that she made the beds. Then she cut some cold meat and made sandwiches. Next she opened a jar of jelly. She also put on the table what was left of the cake Carmela had baked day before yesterday. She stood off from the table and took a good look at the luncheon she had put together for the men. She decided it would do.

She hurried out of the house and toward the horse barn. Ann was fed up with housekeeping. For days now, all she had done was cook and wash dishes for hungry men. She wanted to get away from it all, and she decided that now when things were quiet at River Ranch would be a good time for her to get away. She had decided to ride up and visit Carmela, who had been alone a night and a day and who would be glad to see her.

Ann had a little trouble catching her horse. His name was Six-bits, and though he was an old and quiet animal, he had not been out of the corral for several days. He had been eating his head off all those days, and now old Six-bits was feeling frisky. He made Ann chase him around the corral three times before he let her catch him.

"Old fool," she said to him as she dragged him toward the barn. "You are just like my old housecoat. I've outgrown both of you. Just because you have something from the time you are a little child does not mean you should have to keep it for the rest of your life. I need a new housecoat. *And* a new horse."

She brushed off Six-bits's back, and the old horse dropped his lower lip and his yellow teeth showed. His eyes drooped and he started to drop off to sleep. Ann, giving a strong push with the brush, felt him swaying on his feet. There was nothing Six-bits liked better than a brushing, unless it was food. At last he was ready for the saddle. No sooner had Ann placed it on his back than he began to puff out his sides. Six-bits did not like a saddle to fit too tightly. So now Ann had to bring her knee up and punch him in the ribs to make the saddle fit at all. But at last she got it fastened tightly enough not to slide off his back when she mounted him. Next she had to put the bit in his mouth. Six-bits was very good at taking care of this too. He had a long neck, and as soon as Ann tried to get the bit between his teeth Six-bits stretched up his neck as far as it would go. It went a long way above her reach. But Ann had been going through this with Six-bits for years. She was almost used to it.

She reached into her shirt pocket and brought out a piece of sugar. With her hand opened out flat, she held the sugar toward him. At once Six-bits lowered his nose, and his long lips moved gently over Ann's hand. Quick as a flash, she shot the bit between his teeth. Now he was caught. In another minute Ann was in the saddle and riding out of the corral.

She had decided to give herself a nice long ride today. So she had planned to ride to Juan's rancho by the road. She could return home over the back trail and get there in plenty of time to make supper.

She had left a message for Ben telling him where she was going and when she thought she would be back. There was nothing she needed to be worried about. The day was fair, and she was out to have a good time. As good a time, that is, as anyone could ever have with Six-bits.

Six-bits seemed to be having a good time too. He pointed his ears and lifted his feet proudly. Once, when a bunch of dry grass came rolling toward them, he forgot he was no longer a colt and hoppity-hipped into the air as lightly as a rabbit. But after a mile or so his friskiness wore off, and he settled down into the thumping trot which had become a favorite with him over the years.

Just beyond the Horton place Ann came to the road leading off from the highway toward Juan's rancho. One could hardly call it a road. It was only two tracks cut into the dry grass by the wheels of Juan's cart. Six-bits chose the wider of the two tracks and followed it without need of a signal from Ann.

Birds made a busy sound in the brush along the roadside. Once a jackrabbit bounced up the road ahead of them, and Ann was glad Danger had not come along. He would have been off after it, howling and barking in the way dogs have when they chase rabbits. On and on they went, Ann and Six-bits, in and out and round about the mountain. Now and then, as the road turned, she could look down and see the valley far below. She could pick out the buildings on River Ranch. She could see the river shining in the distance. She could see the tumble-down buildings of the Bar-B outfit. No life was stirring on that ranch. Ann wondered, as she had often wondered in times past, just how the Horton brothers were able to hang on from year to year. They never seemed to work.

Six-bits had long ago slowed to a walk, as the road

began to climb the mountain. Slower and slower his walk had become, until, all at once, he slowed down to a full stop.

"Get up," said Ann, "you can feast your eyes on the valley when we get to the top. I have not got all day for this trip."

Six-bits took a long breath and very slowly began to move again. But his stopping had brought Ann's eyes back to the little road. She had thought that perhaps there was something in the road which Six-bits was afraid of. She had seen nothing, and so she had told him to step along. But as he started to move, something in the road did catch her eye. What was suddenly different about the track they were following? She pulled up on the bit, and the horse stopped as if frozen. There were some signals which Six-bits never needed to have twice. It was well he had stopped so quickly. Another step, and he might have wiped out the thing Ann had noticed. But now it lay, wide and telling, straight across the path. It was the track of a smooth automobile tire!

Ann sat without moving for a full minute while thoughts raced through her head. Whose tire track was this? Juan didn't have an automobile. She was sure Ben had not driven up this way. Another thing: this track was going across the road. It was plain that the truck, or car, had come carefully up the road in Juan's own tracks and then at this spot it had turned suddenly across the road.

Ann followed the track with her eyes. It led to the edge of the road. But what was it doing there? There was only brush alongside the road. There was no other road leading off at this spot. There was no other place it could lead off to!

Ann got off Six-bits. He was a Western horse, and she knew he would stand without being tied. It might be safer to tie some horses, even Western horses. Ben never took a chance with Pilot. But she knew she wouldn't have to be worried about Six-bits running away. Whatever his faults might be, he was a nice safe animal!

Carefully she went to the edge of the road. Slowly

she parted the dry, dusty branches of brush. On the other side of them, going downward at a very sharp pitch, was something that might be called a road. Without thinking of any danger, Ann walked quickly down it. Rocks turned under her boots. There were deep holes and cuts where water had run off the mountain when it rained. But the road was wide enough to hold a car, and there were plenty of signs that a car had been over it.

This is fun, Ann thought as she went swinging along. More fun than dreaming along on Six-bits. I came out to have a good time, and I am even having an exciting one.

Down, down she went until she thought she must have gone almost a half a mile. Suddenly the way took her around a large clump of brush and then it seemed to end. She stood puzzled for a minute. The road had led to nowhere! She turned and stared at the pile of brush. The leaves on it were not fresh. There was something funny about that pile of brush. Quickly Ann stepped toward it. She pulled at a branch, and it came loose in her hand. She grabbed another, and another. Now something was showing under the brush. Carefully she reached in her hand and felt around. Her fingers came up against steel. She threw off more brush. And now she could see what was under it. A pickup truck! It had been covered with the brush to hide it!

She got down and looked at the tires. They were old tires. They were quite smooth. Ben had told her that the truck tracks at the killings had been smooth. This was the truck. It must be the truck.

She straightened up. She looked at the bed of the truck. There was a heavy piece of cloth rolled up in the back. It might be the covering they used to hide the meat. Ann looked closely at it. There was something dark on it, a spot of reddish brown. There was a big spot on the bed of the truck.

Her heart was beating fast. She had found the truck the cattle killers used. She must hurry home and tell Ben. When they found out to whom this truck belonged, they would know who the cattle thieves were.

Suddenly she heard a voice behind her. "Hands up!"

For one-half a minute Ann thought of running. She didn't know what to do. Maybe she should look around first before she did anything. Maybe that voice was only playing with her. Slowly she turned. What she saw made her draw in her breath quickly. Her face went white.

As Ann turned around she found herself looking into the barrel of a blue-black six-shooter. A man was holding it straight toward her. The man was Fred, the River Ranch cowhand.

"Hands up!" said Fred again in a voice that was clear and mean.

Without a word, Ann slowly lifted her hands into the air.

CHAPTER NINE

Where Is Ann?

WHEN Ben came into the kitchen at lunch time and found Ann's message, he picked it up and read it. He looked over the top of the letter paper at the food Ann had fixed for him.

"They don't come any better than Ann," he said out loud.

"You have spoken truth," a voice said behind him. Juan was standing in the doorway, his old battered hat in his hand. "Did she run away?"

"Looks like it," said Ben, drawing out a chair. "But she made sure first that we were well taken care of. She's quite a girl, is our Ann."

Juan sat down, and the two of them ate as only people who work out of doors ever eat.

For the rest of the afternoon, whenever he could, Ben kept an eye out for Ann. In his heart he knew that if she had told him of her plans, he would not have let her ride off by herself. And he thought that Ann had known this when she decided to go without saying something about it first. Until the cattle killers were caught, it was just as well to be careful. Somewhere in this valley there were some bad men at work. Ben didn't want Ann to run into them.

By five o'clock he knew she should be home, and it was time to do the evening work around the barn anyway. He was glad to have something to take him to the house. He wanted to know for sure that Ann had returned home safe and sound.

But as he came nearer to the house, he saw no signs that anyone was getting supper there. No smoke was coming out of the kitchen chimney as it always did about this time of day. A little fear began to tighten around Ben's heart. Then he rounded a corner of the barn, and his heart gave a great jump at what he saw. Standing near the back door, with the saddle still on his back, was Six-bits. Something in the way the horse stood there frightened Ben. He was sure that, even though Ann might have come home late, she would first stop to take the saddle off her horse and turn him into the corral.

He got off Pilot and hurried into the house. Sure enough, there was no one there. He went from room to room, calling. There was no sign that Ann had been home at all.

Ben returned to the kitchen and picked up Ann's message. Yes, it said she had gone to Juan's rancho. She didn't say whether she had gone by the back trail or by the road. But they never rode their horses to Juan's rancho by the road. Or almost never. Surely Ann had taken the back trail.

Anything might have happened to her, Ben kept telling himself as he went out and swung into Pilot's saddle again. Six-bits might have slipped on the trail and fallen, throwing Ann. It was not very likely, however. Ann was a fine rider, and Six-bits was a very safe animal. Still there was always a chance that something like that might have happened.

Then, too, Six-bits might have just decided to come home without her. At this very minute Ann might be sitting safely at Juan's rancho with Carmela, waiting for Ben to come and get her. He knew that Ann always let Six-bits stand without tying him. He had never come home without her before in all these long years. But there was a chance that it might have happened. No use thinking right off, Ben told himself, that she had run into the cattle thieves. That sort of thing happened only in moving pictures. No use getting all upset until he knew what had happened.

Thinking of these things, Ben rode in search of Juan. When he found him and told him about what had happened, Juan was not as frightened as Ben.

"Something has happened to her," he said, pulling

on his pipe, "but it cannot be the cattle thieves. Have you forgot they are now at the other side of the valley at Red Casey's?"

"I thought of that," said Ben. "But you can't feel safe as long as they are in the valley at all. I think we should ride up the back trail before it gets any darker. If she has been thrown and is lying somewhere with a broken leg, it will not make things easier to have it dark when we find her."

"You are right," said Juan. "But have you forgot about the cattle in the lower pasture? Do you think it wise to leave them without anyone to look after them? Use your head, Ben. That is what you have it for."

Ben looked worried. "The little fool," he said at last. "Why did she have to pick a time like this to go running off? Why couldn't she have stayed put for another day or so?"

"You are saying that because you are afraid," said Juan, and he smiled wisely at Ben. "In your heart you know that she did nothing bad. No one can work all the time without some play. It has been hard for Ann."

"I suppose you are right," said Ben. "And I guess there is no point in your riding up the back trail with me. Put Six-bits back into the corral, will you? If I find Ann, I'll lift her onto Pilot and lead him home. I'll be gone for some time, Juan. But you won't have any trouble tonight. As you say, the killers are working the other end of the valley. But just the same, *keep an eye on our herd!*"

"I will," promised Juan.

In another minute Ben was off in a cloud of dust as Pilot raced toward Juan's rancho.

But Ben did not find Ann lying helpless along the back trail. It was growing dark by the time Pilot's hoofs went clopping across the little wooden bridge. He saw lights from Carmela's kitchen window shining through the trees. He hoped with all his heart that Ann was safe inside.

The dogs started to bark as he rode into the yard. He got off Pilot and knocked at the door.

"Who is there?" called Carmela.

"It's me—Ben."

He heard her turn a key in the door, and then Carmela was standing in front of him, her kind fat face filled with worry.

"What is wrong, Ben?"

"Is Ann here?"

Slowly Carmela shook her head. "I have not seen her since I came home from River Ranch."

For a minute the two stood and looked into each other's eyes. Then Carmela reached out and took hold of the front of Ben's shirt. She began to shake him just as she used to do when he was ten years old.

"What have you done with Ann?" Carmela was crying now. "Tell me, what have you done with my Ann?"

Gently Ben backed her into the kitchen and sat her down in a chair. "Get hold of yourself, Carmela. I have not done anything with Ann. She started up here on Six-bits this afternoon, and at five o'clock I found the horse standing in our dooryard and no

Ann anywhere around. I thought she had come up here by the back trail and might have had something happen to her on the way. But I have just come over the trail without seeing a sign of her. So now I am going to ride home the way I came and start back up the road in the truck."

"Something has happened to her. Something bad. I feel it here. It is plain." Carmela laid a fat hand over her heart and looked at Ben, her eyes swimming with tears. "I go with you."

"You will do nothing of the kind," said Ben.

"I say I go with you." Carmela was reaching for her coat, which hung on a nail on the back of the kitchen door.

"Carmela!" Something in Ben's voice made Carmela stop. "Carmela, you are going to stay right here. If Ann is anywhere near, she will try to get to this house tonight. You are going to stay and be here if she does come."

That settled it. Without another word, Carmela hung the coat back. "Very well, Ben," she said quietly. "I shall stay and say prayers for you both."

"Thank you, Carmela." Ben put an arm around the old woman's shoulders and hugged her hard.

In another minute he had left the house, and Carmela could hear the clopping of Pilot's hoofs on the wooden bridge.

It was lucky Red had sent the pickup truck home yesterday, Ben was thinking as he slid Pilot down the back trail. He rode like a wild man. Pie seemed to know how Ben was feeling, for he needed no signal from his rider to go as fast as he could. Many and many a time he had to sit and slide on his tail where the trail went downhill sharply. But he knew every inch of it and was as sure-footed as a mountain goat.

At last they were out of the hills and racing across the grassland of River Ranch. As he came in sight of the house, Ben was happy to see lights in it. Then Ann had got home, after all! He spoke to Pilot, and the pony seemed to fly over the ground. He slid to a stop by the back steps, and Ben was out of the saddle and up the steps in two jumps.

He was in too big a hurry to see that there was another pickup truck standing near the steps. His one thought was of Ann. If he saw the truck at all, he thought of it only as the one which had brought her home. Great was his surprise, then, when he entered the kitchen, to find Red Casey and two other ranchers standing in it.

"Red!" said Ben at sight of his friend.

"I have some bad news for you, Ben."

Ben just looked at him and waited for the blow to fall.

"Fred is gone."

"Fred!" Ben said the name over as if he were too stupid to remember whose name it was. But inside him he was thinking, Thank goodness the bad news was not about Ann. Then he asked Red, "What do you mean 'gone'?"

"I mean he has struck out for parts unknown. He just isn't around here any more."

"When did he go?" asked Ben.

"Some time last night."

"Well, I'll be—" Ben began. Then he remembered the other two ranchers, one of whom was Windy Smith. He crossed the kitchen to shake hands with them.

"What has been happening around here, Ben?"

"Have you talked to Juan yet?" Ben asked.

"No," Red answered. "We got here only a few minutes ago. Where's Ann?"

Ben told them about Ann.

"Guess it's a good thing we got here. I've told all the ranchers along the highway to be on the lookout for your cowhand," said Red. "Tell me, Ben. Did you ever think that Fred might have been one of the killers?"

Ben shook his head. "No," he said. "Do you think I would have sent him up to your place if I had thought so? And anyway, how do you know he is?"

"Well," said Red, "there was a cattle killing at my place as soon as he got there. And just about as soon as I get back there with a few men from the patrol, he lights out for other places. It looks pretty clear to me that he is the boy we are looking for."

Ben looked down at the kitchen floor for a minute. He didn't like to think of Fred as a cattle thief. But it did begin to look as if he were the one. And now Ann was gone. On the very day that Fred had left Red Casey's too. Was Fred somehow mixed up in this?

"Better get going," said Red. His face looked mean. It would not go well with Fred if the two men were to meet tonight. "The first thing is to find Ann. If anything has happened to her . . ."

Red didn't finish what he was about to say. But the men who heard him knew what was in his head. Together the four of them left the kitchen.

"One of you fellows take my truck and tell the five nearest ranchers to come at once to River Ranch," said Red. "Smith, saddle one of the horses over there"—he pointed toward the horse barn—"and go down to the lower pasture." He waved an arm toward that part of River Ranch. "Juan is there riding herd on a bunch of cows about ready for shipping. You stay with him until we come for you. Ben and I will take the other truck and go look for Ann."

The first stop they made was at the Horton place.

"You don't think Ann can be here, do you?" asked Ben.

"No, I don't," Red answered. "But we can't pass up any place. From here to there, we must ask everywhere. Perhaps Hank has seen her since you have. It would help to know. Remember, she must be somewhere. Alive or not."

"Who would want to kill Ann?" asked Ben.

"Nobody," said Red. "But she might have come upon something she wasn't supposed to know about. And somebody might have wanted to be very sure she didn't tell anyone else about it. There is just one sure way of closing anybody's mouth."

Ben swayed in his seat. "I never thought of that," he said. Now, for the first time in his life, he knew what it was like to be really afraid.

The Bar-B house was dark. The Bar-B dog

barked a little when they stopped the truck. Ben jumped out and took the back steps in one jump. He banged on the back door and waited. The Bar-B dog stopped barking and seemed to be waiting now, as were Ben and Red. There was no sound from inside the house. Ben banged again. Still no sound.

"Guess they're not at home. Come on," said Red.

Without saying anything, they returned to the highway. When they came to the little road leading to Juan's rancho, Ben slowed down. He slipped the truck into second, and they began going slowly up the road. Now and then they stopped and called. In the quiet of the night their voices seemed strangely loud. But there was no answering girl's voice to lighten their hearts. On they went, up and up.

The headlights of the truck fingered the spot where Ann had gone off the road and down the hill-side. The brush was still standing as it had been when she parted it to go down. Up and up the game little truck climbed. At last they drove into Juan's door-yard.

Carmela threw the back door open as soon as the truck stopped. "Have you got Ann with you?" she called.

"No, Carmela," Ben answered. "Have you?"

"No, no, no," cried Carmela, covering her face with her hands. Then she dropped them suddenly to shout at Ben. "Go on! Go on, I say. Why you sit there and do nothing? Go on and find my Ann at once."

"Okay, Carmela." Without another word, Ben turned the truck and roared out of the yard.

They made the trip back in nothing flat. As they neared the end of the little road Ben said, "I'm going back to the ranch to see if she may have come home while we were gone."

"Good idea," the older man answered.

Suddenly, to Ben's surprise, Red reached over and, quick as a flash, stopped the engine. At the same time he put out the truck lights.

"What's the big idea?" Ben asked as the truck rolled to a stop.

"Listen!" Red said.

Ben listened. From out of the night rolled the sound of an automobile. It seemed to be coming from the Bar-B ranch.

Red spoke low beside him. "There is a truck pulling into the Bar-B ranch yard, but it isn't coming off the highway. It's coming from the river. See it? Look over by the barn."

Ben looked. For a minute he could see nothing but the dark shadow which was the barn. Then he saw a smaller shadow move out of the large one. It was a truck, traveling without lights.

It stopped, and now the night was again still. But even as Ben watched, wondering what was going to happen next, a shot broke the quiet. There was an answering shot and the sound of lead on steel.

Ben started the pickup.

"I'm going over there," he shouted to Red. "Whatever is happening, I want to know what it is!"

"You took the words right out of my mouth," Red shouted back. "Let her roll!"

CHAPTER TEN

Roundup

THEY drove without lights up the road leading to the Bar-B ranch. There had been no more shots, and the sound of the truck had also stopped. All at once something whistled past the pickup, and another shot rang out.

"Looks like they don't want company," said Red. "What is going on, anyway?"

Ben stopped the truck and turned off the engine. He started to get out of the truck. As soon as he was on the ground, he drew his gun from his belt.

"I don't know what is going on any more than you do," he told Red. "But I'm sure going on in to find out."

"Then that makes two of us," said Red, who had also got out of the truck. Now he crossed over to walk beside Ben. His six-shooter was in his hand.

Carefully they went on, keeping the house between them and the dooryard. At last they were so close they could touch the house. Their eyes had grown used to the dark. They went quietly along the wall of the house until they could see around it into the back yard. There stood the truck they had heard. But no one was in sight.

"The Horton boys must be home now," said Red.

"What makes you think so?" Ben whispered back.

"Because their truck is there."

"But that isn't their truck," Ben said. "Don't you remember the evening Hank came in to join the patrol? He was in the Horton truck then."

"You are right," Red whispered. "I remember now. And this truck has a top on it. Whose do you suppose it is?"

"That is something I plan to find out as soon as I can," Ben answered.

The truck was standing almost in the middle of the back yard, about halfway between the house and the barn. Bending over as close to the ground as he could, Ben suddenly left the shadow of the house and ran toward the truck. At once there was a flash from the truck, the roar of a gun going off, and the thud of lead striking the house. Ben's own gun spoke. At the same time there came an answering roar from the barn. It was followed by the sound of breaking glass. Someone in the barn had shot through the window of the truck.

Now lights began to move along the highway as the men at River Ranch started their cars toward the sound of the shooting. Ben dropped to the ground and hugged it while his eyes tried to see farther into the darkness. Who was in that truck? Someone who didn't want him to come any closer. That much was clear. And who besides himself was shooting at the truck? Were they friends or enemies? He dragged himself carefully through the dirt until he had put an old oil drum between himself and the truck. For once he was glad that the Bar-B dooryard was not as carefully kept as it should have been.

Little by little, and making use of every bit of cover he could, Ben began working his way toward the barn. When he was safely within its shadow, he began moving toward the square of black which was the wide open barn door. When he reached it he stepped quickly inside. He moved as quietly as a cat. No one could have heard him come in.

He could make out the shape of the Horton truck. He went over to it and laid his hand over the engine. It was cold.

That's funny, he thought. It's been less than an

hour since we were here. Could an engine cool off that quickly? Because the Hortons were not at home when we called. He stood for a minute thinking. Or were they? he asked himself.

He turned toward the door again and what he saw made him freeze in his tracks. The shadow of a man was showing against the lighter background of the outdoors. But that was not the thing that made Ben's heart beat so fast. He could see the side of the man's face as he looked into the dooryard. The man was Fred, and he held a gun ready in his hand.

Strange thoughts began to chase themselves around Ben's head. Was Fred a cattle thief? Ben didn't want to think so. Was he the one who had shot at the truck? Or was there another man hidden here in the barn? Then a voice spoke close to his ear and he felt a warm hand on his.

"Ben." It was Ann. "I'm okay, and so is Fred. Oh, I'm so *glad* you are safe here with us."

At the sound of her voice Fred turned. "Who is it?"

"It's Ben," Ann whispered.

"And I have you covered, Fred. Drop that gun before I blow it out of your hand."

"Wait a minute," Fred began, but Ben cut him short.

"You heard me. *Drop that gun!*"

Suddenly there was a brightness outside that made Ben close his eyes as the first of the ranchers' cars swung into the Horton dooryard. It was followed at once by several shots, and when Ben's eyes had got used to the light Fred had gone.

Ben jumped to the door, but Ann reached him and hung on to his arm.

"Don't go out there, you goose," she cried. "The Hortons are in that truck and they'll shoot you on sight."

Ben stopped and looked down at her face. "Are you all right?" he asked.

"Yes," she said. "You see, I found the Horton truck, and then Fred found me, and then—"

"The Horton truck is right there behind me," said Ben. "What are you talking about?"

"Oh dear," Ann said, twisting her hands in helpless anger. "Why are men so stupid? That *is* the Horton truck. But they have two. And the one I found is the one they carry the meat in. Don't you get it?" She began shaking him as if to wake him up. "The Horton brothers are the cattle killers."

"But where does Fred fit into the picture?" Ben asked.

"He's a secret-service man," Ann told him. "He has been watching for weeks to find out who did the killings. Dad sent for him without saying anything to anyone about it. It seems Dad found some cattle killed long before he went away. He watched and said nothing. When it happened again, he sent for help. Fred came. Nothing happened for a while. So Fred told Dad to go away. He thought you might be the one."

"Me!" cried Ben. "That's a likely story! Does he

really think I'm going to swallow anything like that?"

Ben had never been so mad in all his life. So that was the line Fred had fed to Ann. The Hortons might be the killers all right, but if they were, Fred was working right along with them.

"Nuts," said Ben. Brushing Ann to one side, he went through the barn door.

In a flood of headlights, the truck in the middle of the yard no longer held any secrets. Two men sat on the front seat. They were Hank and Andy Horton. In the back of the truck was a load of something covered over with a heavy piece of cloth.

"What do you have in the back of that truck, Hank?" Ben called.

"Why don't you come over and find out?" Hank answered.

No one said anything more for a minute or two. Then Ben heard a man speaking and he knew it was Fred.

"It's no use, Hank," Fred was saying. His voice was quiet, but somehow it seemed to carry a lot of weight. Perhaps Fred had told the truth to Ann. He didn't sound like someone who was working with a pair of thieves. But then Ben remembered the killing at Red's ranch. Surely the Horton boys could not have done that.

"The game is up for you two," Fred was saying. "So far no one has been hurt tonight, although there has been some pretty careless lead-throwing around here. But if you make us take you, someone is going to get killed. So far all we have against you is cattle killing. But if you kill any man here, you will be in much more trouble than you are now. And in the end you will be killed yourselves. Why not come out of that truck with your hands up? You can't win, you know, no matter what you do now. We have you covered, and we don't mean to let you get away."

Numbers of voices joined in to back up what Fred had just said.

At last, very slowly, one from each side of the truck, the Horton brothers jumped to the ground. Then their hands went up into the air.

"Ben," Fred called.

"Here," said Ben, stepping into the circle of light.

"You keep them covered in front while I come up on them from behind. These old boys are a little too foxy to take chances with."

Slowly Ben and Fred began drawing closer to the two thieves. At last they closed in on them, and while Fred went over Hank to make sure that no gun was hidden on him, Ben did the same to Andy.

The men of the Prairie Patrol ringed them round, and Ben stood at last face to face with the men who had killed the River Ranch cattle. Then a thought struck him.

"Were they working at Red Casey's too?" he asked Fred.

The man reached out and laid a friendly hand on Ben's shoulder. "I did that," he said, smiling. "I had to pull your patrol into another part of the valley or we never would have caught these fellows. You were making things altogether too hot for them. They would just have had to lie low until it all blew over.

But not being very bright, and having got away with it so long, they were willing to take chances. As soon as I had taken the hunt away from this end of the valley, I came back to do a little more shadowing. It worked."

"I see it did," said Ben. He didn't look too happy.

Fred understood the way Ben felt. "But the patrol was a fine idea for my purposes," he said. "It covered my tracks and let me work alone as I needed to do. Also, it gave me a chance to size up the ranchers and to decide if any of them might be the men we were looking for."

Ben looked surprised. "You don't think any of these men—" He waved his hand toward the people standing near.

But Fred stopped him. "Even you might have been one of them," he said, smiling at the look on Ben's face. "When I came to River Ranch I came with the understanding that not even you were to know who and what I was. When there are cattle thieves at work, you take no chances of tipping your hand. But I had my eye on these babies almost from the start." He looked at the two whiskered gentlemen before him.

"How come you knew so much?" Hank asked. It was the first he had said since the fight ended. But it was just like him to sound as full of himself now as he ever had.

"Because," Fred answered him, "when people have a place to live and enough to eat and a car to run around in, and they never seem to work at all, you can ask yourself, how come?"

Ann had slipped out of the barn and now slid her hand under Ben's arm.

"If it had not been for me, Fred might never have found out about them though," she said, looking like the cat that ate the canary.

Fred laughed. "That's right," he said. "I was out trying to find out what I could, and I saw Six-bits standing all alone on the road to Juan's rancho. I decided to look a little closer. I followed Ann's tracks down the side of the hill, and pretty soon I found her uncovering this truck." He wagged his head toward the truck the Horton brothers had just left. "And now if you and Red will come along with me," he said to Ben, "I'll take this pair into town. We will let the police take over from there."

"Just a minute," said Ben. "There are still a few things I want to get straight. How did Ann happen to be here in this barn? And is that more River Ranch meat in that truck?"

"One thing at a time," said Fred. None of the others showed any signs of wanting to hurry away. They drew closer as Fred went on with the story of how he caught the Hortons.

"I could not take the chance of letting Ann return home and perhaps tell you about me," said Fred to Ben. "I was sure that by this time you and Red thought I was the man you were looking for, and that no matter what Ann told you, you would not believe it. I could not let you know that I was in this part of the valley. So I made Ann stay with me, even though I knew how worried you would be about her."

Ben remembered what he had been thinking a few minutes ago in the barn and knew that he would not have believed Ann's story if she had come home alone.

"Why didn't you bring her home and tell us yourself?" he asked Fred.

"I had the feeling that the Hortons would strike again tonight. And I was right," he said. "We waited there hidden in the brush. Sure enough, as soon as it was good and dark, here they came on foot to get the truck. We watched them drive away, then Ann and I followed them on horseback. Ann rode behind me as far as the Bar-B. Here we helped ourselves to another horse, and Ann rode with me to the river. We watched them rope and kill two head of cattle while you were gone to hunt for Ann. They didn't trouble to skin them this time. Just cut them up and threw them onto the truck. You will find the pieces under that cloth just as they fixed them there."

"What did they do with the meat after that?"

"That is what I was hoping to find out," said Fred.

"I was going to follow them into town in their other truck and see where they took this stuff. Whoever is buying it from them is just as bad as they are. But my plan was no good because Andy got out of the meat truck and started toward the barn. I knew right away he was going to take the other truck to make it look better if someone should come looking for them. I told him to stand where he was, and he started to shoot it out with me. When I returned his shot, he beat it back to Hank and climbed into the truck beside him again. They stick together, those two."

"I'd have spoiled your plan, anyway," Ben said, "breezing in the way I did. But all I could think of was finding Ann. When I saw that truck moving along without lights, I thought maybe she was in it."

"I'd have done the same thing," said Fred. "You had plenty of sand to walk in here the way you did. And was my face red when you got the drop on me in the barn! I think Uncle Sam could use a man like you in the secret service. Think it over."

Ben smiled. "No, thanks," he said. "As soon as things have quieted down, I'm going to forget all about everything except being a cattle rancher."

Ben let Ann drive the pickup truck to Juan's rancho to let Carmela know that she was safe. She would spend the night there with the old woman and together they would return to River Ranch in the morning.

"Your Dad and Mother will be home by then. We may run into them in town," Fred told her.

"Isn't it *funny*, Ben," Ann rattled on, "to think that Fred got Dad to go away so that he could catch you more easily if it happened to be you. The idea of anybody thinking it could be you!"

"Did Dad think so?" Ben asked Fred.

The older man shook his head. "He knew it was not you. But I didn't. In my game, we don't believe anything until we see it. I didn't want to think you were a thief, but now I don't have to think about it one way or the other. We have caught the thieves. All but one, and I sort of think we'll know who he is before the night is over."

"You mean the fellow that bought the meat from the Hortons?" asked Ben.

"Yes," Fred answered.

Fred was right. Before the night was over, Hank told the police in town all about selling the River Ranch meat to a man who owned a meat market in a city many miles away. He took it from the Hortons and loaded it into his own truck and drove away with it. He bought it from them well under the market price. And they could easily sell it at a low price because it had cost them nothing in the beginning but their time. And the Horton boys always had plenty of that.

It is now several months since the last cattle killing took place at River Ranch. The Horton brothers have been sent away to serve their time. Since then nothing really exciting has happened in the valley.

There have, however, been some changes there.

At River Ranch there are two new hands. One of them is there to take the place Fred left when he went back to being a secret-service man on another job. The second man is riding for River Ranch in place of Ben. No, Ben has not joined the secret service, though he and Fred are good friends.

Ben has his own ranch now. It is just across the river from River Ranch. His father helped him to buy it, and is helping him build up a herd. It is going to be a fine herd of white-faced cattle with red hides, straight backs, and short horns. Ben has given the tumble-down buildings a fresh coat of paint and oiled the windmill. It is beginning to look like a real cattle ranch.

But he has not changed the name or the brand. It is still—you've guessed it—the Bar-B ranch. Ann comes over now and then and puts the house in order. She has been telling Ben about several young ladies in the valley who might do the job as well as she. Of late the River Ranch pickup truck, which Ben sometimes uses, has been making trips quite often to the Quito Ranch where Windy Smith's pretty daughter has seemed quite happy to see Ben. So perhaps Ann will not have to do the housekeeping at the Bar-B very much longer.

Ann's mother brought her a new housecoat for a homecoming present. And in the River Ranch corral there is a brown and white cowpony that nobody rides but Ann. Red Casey trained it for her. He says that Ann and her horse make a mighty pretty pitcher together. So that old struggle still goes on between them.

Pilot likes having the Bar-B corral all to himself. The only one around who is a little unhappy about the way things have turned out is Danger. He can't seem to decide where he wants to live, and has worn a trail between the Bar-B and River Ranch trying to get himself settled.

Juan and Carmela still live at their little rancho among the hills. There Carmela worries for fear something may yet happen to Ann. Sometimes Juan, filling his pipe, stops to wonder how on earth it ever got to that place beside the river where Ben found it that morning long ago. It must have been the work of Andy Horton. But if Andy did plant it there, he has never had a word to say about it. Or about anything else, for that matter.